I've travelled the world twice over,
Met the famous: saints and sinners,
Poets and artists, kings and queens,
Old stars and hopeful beginners,
I've been where no-one's been before,
Learned secrets from writers and cooks
All with one library ticket
To the wonderful world of books.

THE PRIEST'S STORY

It was chance that called Richard Eveleigh to break a cycle journey in Ockenham—a small village near Canterbury, noted for its ancient church and a great house in which the same family has lived for generations. But after his first visit, something happened to Richard. The diffident, slightly discontented schoolmaster gradually became possessed of a purpose which, during the next fifteen years, was to take him from the bachelor security of a private school to a far from easy life in London's East End.

Books by *John Attenborough*
in the *Ulverscroft Large Print Series:*

ONE MAN'S INHERITANCE
THE PRIEST'S STORY

JOHN ATTENBOROUGH

THE PRIEST'S STORY

Complete and Unabridged

ULVERSCROFT
Leicester

First published in Great Britain in 1984 by
Hodder and Stoughton Ltd.,
London

First Large Print Edition
published January 1986
by arrangement with
Hodder and Stoughton Ltd.,
London

British Library CIP Data

Attenborough, John
    The priest's story.—Large print ed.—
    Ulverscroft large print series: general fiction
    I. Title
823'.914[F]   PR6051.T7/

    ISBN 0-7089-1398-9

Published by
F. A. Thorpe (Publishing) Ltd.
Anstey, Leicestershire
Set by Rowland Phototypesetting Ltd.
Bury St. Edmunds, Suffolk
Printed and bound in Great Britain by
T. J. Press (Padstow) Ltd., Padstow, Cornwall

For this trowe I, and say for me
That dreams signifiaunce be
Of good and harm to many wights,
That dreamen in their sleep a nights
Full many things covertly
That fallen after openly.

Geoffrey Chaucer

For
Barbara,
with love

Author's Note

THE village of Ockenham cannot be found on any extant map of the County of Kent, though its contours and characteristics are familiar to many who live in this most beautiful corner of England. Its inhabitants also are born of my imagination, as is Richard Eveleigh whose fate is linked with the men and women of this village.

But there are others, with names recorded in the chronicles of their day, who from time to time step out of their historical context and exert their influence on Richard's life and actions. If in the course of his story, certain saints and sinners present themselves for reassessment, that is purely coincidental to a novel concerned with values more lasting than life or reputation.

J.A.

Part One

THE AWAKENING

What we call the beginning is often the
  end
And to make an end is to make a
  beginning
The end is where we start from.

T. S. ELIOT

1

IT was in the last week of July, 1954 that I first came to the village of Ockenham: and it was there, in the churchyard of Ockenham's ancient parish church, that I first experienced that strange inescapable link with the past which forms the starting-point of this story.

I should explain that in those days I was still resident in East Kent, earning a modest salary as an assistant master at Goldworthy's long-established preparatory school for boys: and my life at this school on the Kent coast was carefree, reasonably happy and totally uncomplicated.

I was not an imaginative type. I harboured no fine thoughts about the future, no speculations on what life was about or why I was born at all. So far as I remember, my mind was a blank except for a strong feeling of resentment at the behaviour of a girl called Mary Winter. That was my state of mind when, at the age of twenty-four, I first came to Ockenham.

But to clarify subsequent events, I need to be a little more precise about my background. My full name is Richard Brooke Eveleigh. Height six feet: weight eleven stone: education Dulwich and Oxford (second class honours): religion C. of E. (nominal only): unmarried. Such were the basic facts recorded on my National Service papers. The details were still true when I left the Army without a commission, and prepared to enter my mother's family business. Nothing significant happened in those two years in the Army except that, by failing to win a commission, I met a variety of "other ranks" from every corner of England who had as little confidence in themselves as I had.

To complete the picture let me add that I am clean-shaven, my eyes are a nondescript grey, and my health is good. So much by way of introduction. You will perceive that the competitive type of education which my parents chose for me has left me in no doubt that I am a "middle of the order" man, scoring no better than "Beta" in any subject or any sport or anything you like to name. You cannot find my name on any Honours Board.

Still, I must tell you something about my family name. Father used to say that the Eveleighs could be traced back a long way to some yeoman family in Kent. But he never produced a shred of evidence to prove it and he died while I was still at school. Maybe this yeoman talk was just one of his fantasies. He told a good story and was at heart an artist: I still have some charming water colours he painted on holiday. Or perhaps in his inconsequential way he was operating some obscure defensive mechanism to convince me that an Eveleigh was as good as a Brooke any day of the week.

There was, you see, nothing chancy about my Christian names. Richard and Brooke were the two names of my maternal grandfather. Mother was his only child: and I suppose it was natural that she should want to preserve the Brooke name.

But there was more to it than that. Old Richard Brooke was also the boss of a paternalistic firm of soap manufacturers with a history stretching back over three generations. Traditionally, Brooke's Factory Soaps Ltd. was a firm in good standing. It paid its hundred and fifty employees slightly more than other un-skilled workers on Thameside. It looked after its people in retirement: and it also provided a steady income for a succession of Brookes who tended to invest their profits in safe gilt-edged securities.

There was nothing, you must under-stand, speculative about the Brooke family. Steady and solid people they were: as lack-lustre and colourless as the factory soap produced in their out-of-date factory. Brooke's Factory Soap was still the same shape, the same colour, the same smell and —give or take a little—made from the same ingredients that the first Richard Brooke had found suitable for Victorian factories in the 1850s. My mother was in no way different from the rest of her family.

My father, Tom Eveleigh, entered the Brooke business soon after the First World War. It was, I fancy, the only job he could get, but he was certainly a cut above the rest of the staff. Old Brooke was entirely happy when he courted and married my mother. And when I appeared on the scene in 1930, my grandfather reckoned that Brooke soaps were good for another generation, and gladly paid for my expensive education—something that neither his own family nor my father had ever enjoyed.

There were, however, certain snags which finally wrecked this solid piece of family planning. First, my father died in the late thirties. Secondly, old Brooke died of sheer fatigue stemming from the 39–45 war in which half the Erith factory had been destroyed. Thirdly, when the Army returned me to civilian life, I could think of nothing more depressing than making soap for a living.

In the end, outside forces decided the issue. In 1954 it belatedly dawned on my mother that there were bigger and better soap-makers than Brooke's Factory Soaps Ltd., and she concluded that if the firm did not sell out quickly it would be sunk without trace—and no compensation either for the ageing workforce or for the family.

The sale of the old business was successfully negotiated by our solicitors and accountants and the terms obtained by these excellent people were not ungenerous. But I, Richard Brooke Eveleigh, had been christened to no purpose. I was unemployed and without prospects of income except for a small allowance from my mother.

Being a widow's only child is not an easy relationship. In such a situation—oh yes, I've seen it many times since—the mother either dotes or dictates. My mother, being perforce a shrewd business woman, dictated. On and on she went till I thought I should scream.

"You must make up your mind, Richard. You must be sensible. The accountants have a place for you and are sure they can get you through the Chartered Accountancy exams."

Or a little later, "I've been talking to our solicitors, Richard. Mr. Ruthven knows a senior manager in the Midland Bank who says the prospects are excellent for a boy with your education."

Luckily, in the 1950s, jobless men with my educational background still had one certain escape route. I took it. After a ghastly lunch-time harangue in the small house in Maidstone which mother had bought after the sale of the family business,

I left home and signed on as an assistant master at a school on the Kent coast, officially called Cliff's End, but more often known as Goldworthy's, after the name of its headmaster.

There was, of course, no future to the job. I had no teaching qualifications, and I had no money to buy myself into a partnership. But for the time being, I welcomed the start of each new term as a blessed escape from my mother's voice. It was entirely coincidental that I was also happy teaching the small boys.

Soon, however, I found an additional attraction at the school in the person of this fair-haired girl, Mary Winter. She was some years my senior, old enough to have wartime nursing experience in Cairo. Though she said little about those war years, the staff were convinced that some emotional upset while on overseas service had caused her to give up professional nursing and apply for the matron's job at Goldworthy's school. What I know for certain is that she was a great success as a matron, her charm and good looks masking a natural gift of authority. She possessed an intuitive skill in recognising which boys were shooting a line and which were genuinely ill or unhappy. But she also had no favourites, treating them all with equal good humour. She was as popular with the boys as with the staff; and she could even handle over-fussy parents without giving offence. All in all, she played a considerable part in the life of the school and old Goldworthy was lucky to have her on his staff. Good matrons are rare birds in boarding schools.

My first meeting with Mary outside the school occurred casually enough when she offered me a lift to the beach in her battered two-seater. I knew others were competing for her favours, notably Keith Figgis, a good-looking athlete of splendid physique who seemed to be endowed with everything that women wanted. But Mary did not cut me out. On the contrary, she seemed to prefer my company. And this was strange because I had always been nervous in women's company—a legacy, I suppose, of my only-child, mother-dominated upbringing. Truth to tell, I always felt a fearful inadequacy when listening to the sexual exploits of my barrack-room mates.

Somehow, Mary arranged for her off

duty times to coincide with mine. On hot days—and there were many of them in 1954—we often swam together near the rocks at the end of a bay close to the school. Swimming with her and drying off afterwards, it was impossible not to be aware of the nearness of her lithe, beautiful body, her skin honey-coloured in the sun's glow. I was excited by her smile when she turned her head towards me, with her eyes full of inquiry, as if sizing me up. Lazily she would ask questions about myself and my home. She knew the staff gossip—was it true that I taught maths as well as history? What did I think of old Goldworthy? And so on—a catalogue of questions with me supplying the answers. Our relationship was all simple, innocent, relaxed, unhurried.

Then one day, her eyes and mouth teasing me, she said in that lazy half-mocking voice of hers, "Do you know, Richard, I believe you're just like every other mother's boy. Afraid of girls, aren't you? Afraid of me? Afraid to make love?"

She couldn't have spoken a truer word. But it was the way she said it that turned me up. I hardly knew what happened next.

Before she could say another word, I had hit her as hard as I could, my right hand making an angry mark on her thigh. I didn't care a damn. She'd provoked me. She'd caused the flare-up. It was her fault and I meant to hurt her. Who can explain these things? Somehow, she wriggled free of my grip and instead of losing her temper she twisted onto her back and pulled me towards her, smothering me with kisses. For a moment, she held my head in her hands, her eyes sparkling and her lips alive with invitation.

"So you're a wicked old wife-beater, are you," she whispered, "not a mother's boy at all, not even a stuffed dummy of a maths teacher. Now, it's my turn to do the teaching." So we made love for the first time, naked under the sun . . .

Later, I lay fulfilled and happy beside her, and she bent over me again and said, "Thank you for proving I'm wrong about mother's boys. Don't mathematicians always conclude their proof with 'QED'?" I no longer felt inadequate.

That was the start of the affair. After our first tempestuous meeting we made love many times—twice, rather dangerously, in her bedroom at the school. In our own way, we tried to be honest with each other. She told me that other men had made love to her and I accepted that I was no more than her latest and youngest lover. If she found pleasure in my inexperience, what of that? She'd done something for me—removed my sense of inferiority, almost given me the feeling that I was a better man than the other people on the staff. We were happy in each other's company and light of heart.

By the end of the term, I could not bear the idea of leaving her. Walking with her in the woods behind the school, I asked her to join me on holiday and I suggested we get engaged. It was only then that she drew back, adamant in her refusal to take the affair any further.

"Not so fast, my handsome mathematician," she said, "not so fast. Short cuts in life never work. You go away and think things out, Richard. I'll do the same, but no promises, see? We've extracted a lot of fun from school life, but let's stay fancy free till next term." And with that she kissed me lightly on the mouth and turned away.

There may have been tears in her eyes, but she never looked back.

I was, therefore, thoroughly out of sorts when I made for home at the end of term and reached the Wotton Arms in Ockenham with a bicycle and rucksack as my only companions. Ockenham, as you may know, is a small village situated some ten miles west of Canterbury, just off the main road to Maidstone. Apart from the pub, it still has a church, a school, a general store, and a Post Office: and at the end of the village, a lodge guards the entry to a magnificent beech avenue leading to a great house which, together with the surrounding land, has been owned by the same family for hundreds of years. From a small hill opposite the Lodge gates an ancient church looks down on the village and the water meadows beside the Stour, its squat Norman tower so strong that I reckon it must have been built primarily for the defence of the first Norman invaders rather than for the glory of God.

The Wotton Arms lies at the Canterbury end of the village. My fellow schoolmaster, Keith Figgis, had recommended it to me. "Shepherd Neame from the wood, Richard: served in excellent condition. And the innkeeper's wife is one of the best cooks round Canterbury." It seemed a good port of call before returning to Maidstone for a further catechism of questions from mother.

So here I was on this lovely July day, trying to forget Mary Winter with the help of good Kentish ale and a home-made snack served by a dark-eyed Italian girl who proved to be the innkeeper's wife. The bar was not crowded at midday and I soon began to pick up a few facts about the village from the local drinkers. The innkeeper, Ted Baker, proved to be an ex-sergeant major who, like his Welsh friend at the garage opposite, had served in the Italian campaign with the present owner of the great house.

The garage proprietor, Evan Morgan, needed little encouragement to talk about the local squire.

"Major Mortimer-Wotton, yer know. A mighty fine soldier, eh, Ted?"

"Ay, that's right, Evan bach. The best officer I ever served with. And no side to him, either."

They included me in the conversation.

"If you've a moment to spare, sir, you might like to see where the Major lives. Just climb the hill to the church. You'll get a good sight of the Great House from there. The front has just been rebuilt—bust open by a stray German bomb in forty-three. Come to think of it, you might be interested in the church too. It attracts a lot of visitors these days."

"Any special features?" I asked.

"Ay, I reckon it's the brasses. You can read about it in this guide book." Ted Baker handed me a copy. "Put what you like in the box—thank you, sir. Nowadays a lot of people come to see the brasses in the chancel. This brass-rubbing craze, I'd say, will finish off Sir Thomas Mortimer and the Lady Edwina unless parson puts a stop to it."

"True enough," the Welshman added. "But there's other things up there too— the roofing, yer know, and some of the memorials to the Major's family. Not surprising really, seeing as how his family built the place originally and still decides

16

who should be parson. Ay, it's got a long story, has our church."

Thomas Mortimer, Lady Edwina, Major Mortimer-Wotton . . . Strange how these chaps at the pub spoke of the dead and the living with a mixture of familiarity and respect, as if they all came within the orbit of their acquaintance . . . Full of such thoughts, I climbed the hill to the church of St. Dunstan.

The Wotton Arms clientele had certainly not oversold the local tourist attraction. Never, I swear, have I seen a more beautiful small parish church. Dominated by the strong Norman tower which first caught my eye, it also has a nave supported by arches and pillars of Norman design. The west door—Norman again—is surrounded by the strangest fancies of some local sculptor in which village worthies and animals are interspersed. And close by is a stone font of unusual design. "Has affinities with Moorish work as seen at Monreale in Sicily," the guide book told me. "According to legend it was brought home by a crusading Mortimer in thanksgiving for the birth of a son." But most exciting of all is the fan-roofing in the chancel and transepts which complete the cruciform plan of the building. Added to the original structure in the fourteenth century, the work, exquisite in design, looks like a miniature of the high vaulting at Canterbury. Without any feeling of surprise, I read in the guide book, "The transepts are known to have been built on the instructions of the Lady Edwina Mortimer (c. 1330–1390) by Henry Yvele, the master mason who was later to become famous for his work at Canterbury."

On that first visit to the church I remember taking a last lingering look at the interior and emptying the contents of my pocket into an alms box. There I stood —a lone intruder into this little world of continuous occupation, surrounded by early Mortimers in stone and brass, and later memorials to the Wotton family. On the war memorial, among the familiar Kentish names, Fagg and Hogben, Pittock and the rest, I saw the name of Mortimer-Wotton. Could their family history, I wondered, ever have been interrupted or its inheritance challenged?

Then, for some reason, I paused to read

the names of the previous incumbents listed in the porch. They sounded to my enchanted mind like music—variations on a single theme. "Randolph de Mortimer, 1250; Henry de Glanville, 1304; Edward of Northbourne, 1316; John Chillenden, 1350; Nicholas Maidstone, 1370 . . ." I paused for a moment, recognising the series of local place names: and then continued with a sort of random recitation, mouthing the words that took my fancy. "Richard Courtenay, William Hardres. John Frebody, 1520" . . . odd way to spell his name, I wonder how he coped with the Reformation. "Thomas Brown, Augustus Scrope DD 1750" . . . sounds as if he carried too much weight for a village church. On and on, without a gap in history till I reached "Interregnum 1941", only to be reassured by the final entry "John Reynolds, 1944".

I emerged into the afternoon sunshine with this peal of names ringing in my ears. I ought to be moving off—it was still thirty miles to my mother's house in Maidstone. But I felt a strange compulsion to stay a little longer. I wandered across the church-yard, and reached a grassy slope rising to a

19

wall of Kentish rag, with a sheer drop on the far side. It was almost like a miniature wall of defence with a surrounding ditch designed to make the assailant's task more difficult.

There I lay, gazing across the valley to the Great House. With its reconstructed front facing me it seemed a modest heritage compared with the great houses of Kent— Hever, Knole, Penshurst or the Inigo Jones masterpiece at Waldeshare. But it had a lion's strength of its own, crouching there in the lazy afternoon and basking in the sun from the south. In front of the house was a rose garden, a profusion of colour surrounded by green lawns. Away to the left were farm buildings: and behind the house, a ridge of wooded high ground acting as a framework for the picture I was contemplating. Further to the right and stretching to the horizon I could see a patchwork of fields under cultivation, with wheat and barley turning golden for the harvest. And in the foreground was a lake and a park with cattle grazing or standing under clumps of beech and oak.

On such a day in high summer, the scene appeared so peaceful as to be out of this world, untouched by the drama of life. Yet in the church behind me evidence abounded of war and tragedy: the squat tower, knights in armour, a memorial to a child who had died of plague, a plaque commemorating the dead of two wars . . .

I must have dozed off. Suddenly those men who had served St. Dunstan down the centuries were parading before me, queueing to catch my eye, jostling with each other and sorting themselves into their historical order. I remember the leader as a tall saintly man to whom I could give no name. He was followed by bearded Victorians and then a vast pot-bellied eighteenth century Divine—Dr. Augustus Scrope for sure. Back, back to a man carrying a girl who seemed to be in a state of trance . . . Back again in history until a young priest, clad in a black monkish habit, broke ranks and confronted me with a fearful cry.

"Woe to the House of Lancaster, he that has silenced Wycliff and killed great Mortimer. Woe to Gaunt's lackeys, those murderers and despoilers of the poor. Do something for the love of Christ." His face was grey with grief. "Can't you understand? They've killed Mortimer's boy most horribly. Who is left to fight for Mortimer? Pity, good sir. Show pity." The young priest came close to me, his hands outstretched and his face full of a hopeless sadness, of grief inconsolable.

I woke abruptly. Clouds obscured the July sun. I was cold and a chill wind was blowing through the gravestones in the churchyard. It was time, high time to be going. I shouldered my rucksack and took to the Maidstone road. Yet I could not travel fast enough to escape my dream. I was constantly aware of the priest stumbling along beside my bicycle, imploring my help.

The sun broke out again over the Kent countryside. As the shadows lengthened on that summer evening, the places and people of an earlier England assumed shape and life in my lonely imagination—people and places that were familiar to the young man by my side. Places . . . medieval Oxford and London and Canterbury: castles like Leeds and Dover and Ludlow. People pleading for recognition and even for reappraisal . . . Chaucer's pilgrims, the Mortimers and their ladies, the Black Prince, Wycliff, Wat Tyler, Richard of

Bordeaux and his grasping villainous uncle, John of Gaunt. And ever returning to the centre of the picture, I was conscious of Ockenham and the succession of priests recorded at the entrance to St. Dunstan's church, and the façade of the Great House where the name of Mortimer was still held in honour.

2

MY one-track mind was still wrapped up in a fourteenth-century dream when, late that night, I reached my mother's terraced house in Maidstone. The inevitably querulous greeting awaited me. "Richard dear, how lovely to have you back. But why so late? Why didn't you ring? I'd been expecting you for tea."

Hell, I thought, I might still be a schoolboy: and like a schoolboy I was reduced to making time-worn excuses. "Late getting away, Mother. A spot of trouble with the old bike. You know how it goes."

In due course, we settled down to tea and digestive biscuits in her small overcrowded living room. She nattered endlessly about the neighbours and the cost of living: and I chipped in with a few inconsequential stories about Goldworthy's school. But I said nothing about Mary: and nothing, of course, about the ghostly character who had met me in the church at Ockenham and joined me on the journey home. It was a relief to say goodnight and slip into bed.

It was only when I surveyed my bedroom —the well-aired sheets neatly turned down, the garden flowers freshly picked, the old books dusted, father's picture standing with mother's on my side table—that I felt thoroughly ashamed of my boorish behaviour throughout the evening.

This sense of guilt is the only reason I can give for suggesting to my mother the following morning that we go on a picnic outing. She was obviously pleased at this idea, and it did not seem in any way strange when she proposed we drive to a destination well-known to both of us from earlier boyhood excursions.

This favoured picnic spot is to be found a few miles south-east of Maidstone on the slope of a hill overlooking Leeds Castle. From this height of land you get a superb view of the mighty fortress which Edward I transformed into a palace for his queen. People will tell you that no spectacle in England is more evocative than the view of this royal residence. There the great castle stands, rising majestic from its surrounding lake amidst the meadows bordering the River Len. When the sun shines, as it shone that day, the battlements are brilliantly reflected in the placid waters which encompass its ancient walls, while nature provides an incomparable background of green pasture land and wooded hills. One cannot escape the impression that in this place, if nowhere else, God and Man met together in some magical act of creation. In such a place history comes easily to life.

Mother and I were sitting on our picnic rug, idly taking in the familiar scene, when I became conscious of a third presence at my side. "Maidstone is the name." The words beat insistently in my ears. "Nicholas Maidstone, you know: the name you saw in the church at Ockenham. I, too, knew this castle in the days of young Richard, the king, when the men of Kent and the Kentish Men joined Wat Tyler's march on London. But I lived here long before that tragedy, many years before I entered Mortimer's household. Born to a village girl and sired by the Prior of Leeds if you really want to know. You'll find his name in the church which stands on the hill above Leeds village."

It sounded like a command. I turned to my mother, noticing almost for the first time her greying hair and the lines of age on her face. She was busy clearing the picnic, preoccupied and unconscious surely of the voice I'd heard. Yet to my surprise, she looked up as if I had spoken to her and casually suggested we return home by way of Leeds village so as to have a look at the church. Don't ask me who put the idea into her prosaic matter-of-fact mind. It could have been coincidence; but I remain convinced that, later on that same afternoon, as I stood in the church of St. Nicholas in Leeds village, my hand rested on the Norman font where, somewhere around 1340, a bastard son of Prior Thomas of Leeds had been christened in the name of the patron saint of church and monastery. And I am no less certain that, when we inspected the sad ruins of the great Augustinian Priory of Leeds in the valley below the hill on which the church stands sentinel, I was close to the lodgings where long ago a village girl had shared the Prior's bed.

As we chugged home in mother's small car, she asked me point-blank what was on my mind. She has always been like this— very direct, no subtlety of approach, over-anxious to know my thoughts. I suppose it's natural for a widow with an only son, but it always provokes me to a sort of antagonism, something I can't really explain or justify. For a moment I hesitated. Then I said, "I think it must be seeing the castle and the church, mother: the king and the prior, side by side, sharing so much land between them, dominating the lives of all the people hereabouts. I've an idea I'd like to know more about their world."

"Well," she replied briskly, "why not ask at the Public Library? Heavens knows we pay enough on the rates. It would be good to see some of our money back." Then she turned to me with one of her rare smiles and added, "I'd love to help you, Richard, if you would let me."

That is how we set out together—my mother and I—to piece together the story of Nicholas Maidstone and his connection with the Mortimer family.

Our research began with three days of

concentrated reading in the Maidstone Public Library, with mother looking up references in the Dictionary of National Biography and me mugging up the history of the period. For this purpose we relied for guidance on the three key names which my ghostly apparition at Ockenham had provided—John Wycliff, John of Gaunt and Mortimer. We also knew the historical time span: roughly 1340 to 1381, as supplied by the lists of priests at Ockenham and Leeds. We quickly established that the Augustinian Order not only included the Priory of Leeds among its religious houses, but also owned many acres of farming land in the stretch of England between Kent and the Welsh Marches where the Mortimers were all-powerful. And we also discovered that in the years on which we were concentrating, John Wycliff was lecturing in the Hall of the Austin Friars at Oxford.

"That's all the information we need," I told my mother confidently after three days of study. "We are now equipped to make a journey to the borders of Wales: and we'll make up a story as we go along."

My mother's face lit up with expectation. She was delighted at the prospect of a holiday. "You sound just like your father," she said. "Tom loved to go on sudden, unplanned holidays, and he loved making up stories, half truth and half imagination. 'Let's pretend' was one of his favourite openings."

That's the point at which Nicholas Maidstone, the priest of Ockenham, became, so to speak, our travelling companion. I introduced him to mother as an eight-year-old boy suddenly ordered by Prior Thomas to leave the Priory at Leeds and make a journey across England to the borders of Wales. "But why should a little boy leave the safety of the Priory so early in life?" my mother asked in her rationalising way. It was just the sort of question I get in my history class at Goldworthy's school.

"Mother," I protested, "you remind me of the older Berners-Levine boy. He's always interrupting my classes with questions for which I have to supply plausible answers. However, if you really must know, I suggest that the Prior was a little nervous about having his personal life investigated by his Superior." I corrected myself. "No, let's be a bit more charitable to Prior Thomas and suppose that he was very fond of his young son and terrified lest he remain at Leeds and die of the pestilence which was sweeping through London and the Home Counties in 1349."

Anyway, we agreed that the journey really happened and a rotund little friar, mounted on a lively bay gelding, was deputed to conduct Nicholas and his mother on their long journey. The boy rode behind his mother astride a broad-backed mare, and in order to secure their link with the house of Mortimer, we made their eventual goal the Augustinian Priory at Wigmore near the Welsh border, which had been lavishly endowed by the Mortimer family and was many miles away from London and the dreaded plague. It must have been rough, slow going for fourteenth-century travellers, compared with our swift car journey on tarmac roads: but what a memorable adventure for young Nicholas and his mother whose lives had previously been confined to the village and Priory of Leeds! The little party met pilgrims from London en route for the shrine of St. Thomas at Canterbury. Their eyes were enchanted by the sight of the multi-coloured flowers in the hedgerows lining the rutted track along which they travelled. They noted the changing landscape of England as they rode towards Herefordshire and the Welsh border. They overnighted at religious houses, directing their course to Reigate, Reading and Wantage: and on through the Cotswolds to Cirencester, Gloucester, Hereford and Leominster.

We, for our part, travelled the same road by car in twentieth-century comfort, reaching Leominster within the day. There we sensed that we were already in Mortimer country, for at the hotel we had evidence that in these parts Mortimer still remains a common Christian name. Next morning, when we stopped for a break at Mortimer's Cross, we imagined our fourteenth-century trio resting their horses at the same spot.

My mother said, "About these Mortimers, Richard. If young Nicholas is to enter their service, he will be concerned with Roger Mortimer and his son, Edmund: both of them, according to their entries in the Dictionary of National Biography, highly trusted soldiers and councillors holding high office under the king and the Black Prince. Yet they hardly appear in the history books. The only Mortimer who makes the headlines is the wicked Mortimer of an earlier generation who rose to be the queen's paramour and was alleged to have engineered the murder of Edward II at Berkeley Castle. If he was such a villain, how comes it that Edward III, who sanctioned the wicked Mortimer's execution, also restored the grandson, Roger, to all the Mortimer lands and titles and lavished many fresh honours upon the family? It doesn't make sense. It seems as if some fourteenth-century Ministry of Information has been actively at work, stressing the evil deeds of the wicked Mortimer and expunging from the record the great deeds and honourable service of his successors."

"Your guess is as good as mine," I replied. "It seems to be every historian's problem. History is so often built up from contemporary chronicles in which the writer has a master to please or a cause to serve. Look at this mighty man who was the Mortimers' most deadly enemy: John of Gaunt, Duke of Lancaster and younger brother to the Black Prince! Powerful and capable, if you like: and handsome as a young man, by all accounts. But, as the years passed, increasingly self-centred in all his actions, greedy, treacherous, interested solely in his own aggrandisement and the acquisition of a kingdom for himself or his son. To think of him in old age mouthing Shakespeare's immortal lines! I doubt whether Gaunt ever had much love for 'this sceptred isle . . . this other Eden . . . this happy breed of men . . . this England'. Certainly, nothing could ring more false in the ears of his contemporaries. Why, the man spent most of his time and all the nation's money in France. I'd say he was the best-hated man in England." I pulled myself up with a jerk. I don't think mother realised why I stopped my tirade so suddenly. But I knew . . . I knew deep-down that I was in some odd way reflecting the anger of a priest six centuries dead.

Our thoughts turned to the youthful Nicholas and his mother and their chaperon. If the three of them also rested at Mortimer's Cross before completing the final stage of their journey to Wigmore, we might be at the place where young Nicholas first caught sight of Roger Mortimer—the victor of Calais returning triumphant to his lovely wife, surrounded by a company of knights and squires and men-at-arms—a thrilling flash-past of chivalry and emblazoned blue and silver. It was an exciting picture. I could imagine the boy's delight as the colourful cavalcade swept past him. But there was no time for further speculation. In any case the boy and his mother were bound to meet Roger Mortimer and his lady on reaching Wigmore.

Later, when we in our turn reached the ruins of the castle and priory, we thought of the boy being instructed by the monks, and after six years' tuition being rec-ommended by them to Roger Mortimer, already a Knight of the Garter and Earl of March and soon to be Warden of the Cinque Ports and Constable of Dover. We imagined the great lord sizing up the lad's ability and arranging for his further education at Oxford so as to fit him for a place as a learned clerk in the king's service. At Oxford, arrangements would be made for Nicholas to lodge with some forty other students at the Austin Friars: and there, of course, he would have his first meeting with John Wycliff.

The pieces of our self-imposed jigsaw puzzle were beginning to fit into their allotted places.

Because the border counties of Hereford and Shropshire were so full of beauty, both in their buildings and in the lush richness of the countryside, we spent a few days motoring round the Mortimer strongholds of Ludlow and Bridgenorth before returning home via Oxford where we had booked rooms at the Randolph.

Up to that point, Nicholas had been for me an excuse for a holiday—something to give coherence and purpose to the journey my mother and I were making. But in Oxford—I know not why—his character ceased to be make-believe. It assumed a sort of reality.

True, one can no longer find in Oxford the Hall of the Austin Friars where once John Wycliff argued his cause: but I swear his spirit lives on.

At night, after the tourist coaches leave

the city and the noise of traffic dies, the dim outlines of the past become strangely clear. It is not difficult to conjure out of the midnight air a medieval walled city with six gates and a street plan centred on the ancient Carfax. St. Frideswide's and the church of St. Mary, even the little church of St. Peter-in-the-East, are already adding dignity to the mean cobbled lanes. The city is smaller, far smaller, than fourteenth-century Paris or Bologna: so small that its walls can no longer contain such a ferment of scholarship or such concentrated questioning of established belief. Soon the flame kindled by Wycliff within this University city is certain to burst out of its six gates to ignite the world beyond its boundaries.

And there, in the Hall of the Austin Friars, I can see the young tonsured priest called Nicholas. He has recently arrived from Herefordshire, already a good Latinist and well-equipped to follow the un-Ciceronian Latin of the Schoolmen. He has quickly mastered the routine instruction in grammar, arithmetic, geometry and astronomy, and is now permitted to study Logic and the three Philosophies.

He stands silent and expectant, in the company of other chosen students, listening spellbound to a 25-year-old theologian from Merton College.

John Wycliff is preaching revolution, though he knows it not. He only knows that logic and dialectical argument have forced him to an absolute conclusion. He has uncovered an infallible touchstone.

"The basis of all truth," he proclaims, "is contained in the Bible: and it can be applied to all the world's problems."

Me, I am standing alone, not four hundred yards from our hotel, half-way between Trinity College and the Martyrs' Memorial. The moon rides high. It is after midnight and college gates are closed. I am deaf to the sound of the occasional car. The stillness of the long Summer vacation governs the night. No under-graduate voices may be heard. Yet I am powerfully aware of the Yorkshire accent of a teacher possessed by some inner fire which gives a peculiar pertinence and cogency to his words.

"Back to the Scriptures," he says. "And where do you find authority for the Church

38

to hold twice as much land as the rest of the people? Where do you find authority for the Church to defy the king? Still less, for the Church to pay dues to a Pope in Rome? And by whose authority does this bishop of Rome claim the right to appoint bishops and abbots, deans and arch-deacons, within the hierarchy of England? Away with these 'possessioners'!"

I am half persuaded that I am one of Wycliff's student audience, facing this soberly dressed lecturer with the long predatory nose and eyes set wide in a face which suggests both obstinacy and auth-ority.

"I tell you more," he continues. "Before I die, the Scriptures will be available in English so that every shepherd in our land may hear Christ's words spoken in the English language. Our Lord's words are for everyman. They are not the perquisite of priests . . ."

The picture fades. The students disperse. I turn towards the Randolph. But beside me walks a fourteenth-century student—or so it seems to me—excited by what he has heard, determined when the moment comes to expound these new truths to any who will listen.

Next morning, my mother and I drove back to Maidstone. We laughed about our story of Nicholas which had given point and purpose to our holiday. We began to speculate what might have happened to our young priest after leaving Oxford. Back to Mortimer's service, no doubt, his mental horizon suitably widened. Probably anxious to convey his Wycliff enlightenment to the Abbot of Wigmore, and even to Roger Mortimer and his colleagues on the Royal Council.

But I did not say much about my midnight walk at Oxford. "Just a quick stroll up the Broad before bed," I said in answer to my mother's question, "and a look at the Trinity gardens in the moonlight." She could not be expected to understand my new-found attachment to Nicholas Maidstone. Indeed, I didn't understand it myself.

There was a letter from Mary Winter waiting on the doormat when we got back to the Maidstone house. It was in reply to an effusion I'd posted before starting on holiday—and it was devastatingly negative. "Forget last term," she said in effect. "I have no regrets and you were a darling lover in a dull world. But I'm sure Ma Goldworthy was getting too nosey. There would have been a load of trouble if I had stayed on at the school. So I've cut the painter and given Goldworthy notice. In any case, it's time for me to get back to serious nursing, probably in London's East End. Don't be too angry with me. I shall miss you too. But I'm sure you'll find yourself another and a better matron! I'm much too old to be taken seriously."

Behind the light-hearted style was as clear a rejection as any girl could give to a man. Yet the absurd truth is that I, who six weeks earlier had thought myself in love, now accepted her decision with a sort of relief. Something—or somebody—was telling me that Mary was talking good sense and we were both well clear of a physical love affair with no future to it. It was time for both of us to look further afield. I dashed off a letter to Mary, and tried to forget our summer-term fling.

"Who is the girl?" my mother asked

intrigued by the writing on the envelope.

"Nothing serious," I replied with a smile. "Just a letter from the school matron telling me she's given Goldworthy notice. It looks as if she's returning to professional nursing. I don't suppose we shall meet again."

3

WHEN a man possesses neither cash nor qualifications it's not so easy to look further afield. Being the sort of indecisive person I am, the start of the new school year found me back at Goldworthy's school—just jogging along for want of something better to do.

Apart from the replacement of Mary Winter by a fifty-year-old woman called Edna Clarke, I could see no change in the place. The school buildings still stood firm against the sea winds, the classrooms fortified as always in September by a liberal application of new paint, the smell of which proclaimed to the local inhabitants that a new academic year had begun.

Extensive playing fields, surrounding the school, continued to be tended by an ageing groundsman who was an integral part of the school life and the ultimate in loyalty.

The boys were at full strength—120 of them—all boarders and most of them arriving from well-to-do homes. Fathers who had attended similar schools in their day and generation continued to pay Goldworthy's exorbitant fees to ensure that their offspring won entry to the same schools at which they had been educated. And the mothers took it all for granted.

Over this tight little kingdom, Harold Goldworthy (M.A.Oxon.) reigned supreme, as sure of his world as were the parents he served: and entirely blind and deaf to the emerging truth that 1945 had sealed the demise of the British Empire as surely as it had settled the fate of Adolf Hitler.

In a grudging sort of way, I admired our headmaster. For all his sixty years and grey hair, he remained young at heart—a man of boundless enthusiasm and uncomplicated mind. Neither he nor his wife ever accepted that the world was changing. They voted Conservative without question and assumed that the staff held similar political views if it held any views at all. Society, as they understood it, was encased in a fixed framework.

But they also personified certain old-fashioned virtues: stability, fairness, honesty, good manners and a simple

44

morality which rubbed off on the boys without conscious effort on their part. Goldworthy's was basically a good school.

Games was the headmaster's strong point —his prowess in his younger days being signalled each day by a change of club tie. If he carried the same colours two days running, the staff and Mrs. Goldworthy knew he was a troubled man. Apart from his sporting achievements, he also taught Latin successfully and, to a handful of scholarship hopefuls, some elementary Greek. Teaching the classics with their exact grammar and limited horizons seemed the natural extension of a character that liked to be governed by fixed rules.

I was far less certain about Ma Goldworthy, as the headmaster's wife was universally known. To the outside world she appeared the ideal partner to her husband—hard-working, efficient and still a good-looking woman, who exercised admirable control over the catering and domestic staff. She knew all the boys personally and made a point of meeting their parents. But on the staff we always had the feeling that she was watching us and judging us. This was not a feeling personal to myself—she never made any insinuations about my brief affair with Mary Winter. No, it was something we all felt; a sort of subtle hostility to the younger members of the staff. I think it stemmed from the loss of her son who had been killed on active service with the RAF. For Ma Goldworthy, there could never be any family succession at the school, and no aspirant for the headship could ever be quite good enough.

Those of us who lived in a house on the far side of the playing fields were equally sensitive to Ma Goldworthy's all-seeing eye, and therefore a little nervous of the fifty-year-old Edna Clarke who had been appointed to succeed Mary Winter as matron. The woman was capable enough and brought to the job considerable experience obtained in similar school appointments. But it seemed to our suspicious minds that part of Edna Clarke's brief was to keep a watch on our private out-of-school activities. By half term we were sure that Aunt Edna was no friend of ours.

The headmaster, for his part, was reasonably indulgent towards the staff and receptive to our suggestions. In such matters he was impelled by a spirit of one-upmanship in a private war he enjoyed waging with other schools in the neighbourhood. Thus he encouraged a newly arrived music teacher when she asked permission to organise a voluntary recorder class among boys who had hitherto evinced little interest in music. "An excellent idea, Mrs. Ashcroft," he said, "but remember—no interference with prep. or compulsory games. I know these little blighters. They'll put their noses through any escape hatch which lets them off something they don't like doing."

He was equally helpful to me when I proposed an outing to Dover Castle for the eight members of my top history form. "Excellent, Richard, excellent. It may give them a few new ideas. Take the minibus. Leave at midday with a packed lunch and be back for tea. Right? Make it Wednesday, will you? No games that day. I'll speak to Mrs. Goldworthy about the food." And the old man stretched for his memo pad and noted the arrangement in his impeccable handwriting.

On the following Wednesday, the twelve-year-olds and I reached Dover Castle and armed ourselves with guide books. Was it coincidence, I wondered, that on scanning the long list of Constables, I immediately spotted the name of Roger Mortimer? Until this moment, the daily chores of school life had kept me free of my holiday obsession. Now, the Mortimer family and their henchmen were again intruding on my mind. I turned the page to study the plan of the huge castle, conscious that my studies in the Maidstone Public Library had made me familiar with at least one episode in Dover's history.

After a quick tour of the outer fortifications and a visit to the ancient church of St. Mary-in-Castro, we collected the packed lunches from the minibus and climbed to the top of the central tower of the castle. We demolished the school food at remarkable speed, sitting on the step below the parapet, with the October sun shining out of a blue sky, a light breeze blowing from France and the rhythmic noise of the sea breaking against the white cliffs a thousand feet below.

Then, with the empties tidily stored in a litter bin, the normal puppy scuffling started. "That's my place, Anderson." "No, it's not.""Well, budge up then." "Get off my foot, can't you?" And then the inevitable question: "What do we do next, sir?" The question came from Daniel Berners-Levine, a boy who did not really fit the school's social pattern, being the son of a property tycoon who'd come up the hard way. It was time for serious business.

"Right," I said, "I'll tell you a story, and you want to listen as it may give you ideas for the essay you have to write tomorrow morning. Everybody ready? Let's start.

"You've looked at the guide books, so you've got the shape of the castle in your minds and you know it was built by King John and developed by his successors. We've reached the fourteenth century— name the kings, Brown."

"Henry, sir?"

"No, rotten shot, you're centuries off target. Help him, somebody. OK. Berners? Yes, the Edwards, one, two and three— and the last of them determined to win the French crown. We're slap in the middle of the Hundred Years War with France.

"We'll throw in a few dates for good measure. Put them in your notebooks. The

French beaten at Crecy, 1346—good. And the great plague which stopped the fighting, 1349. But these Plantagenet kings —spell it somebody—are determined to be kings of France as well as England. Not only the old king: but his famous son, the Black Prince who is the greatest soldier in Europe: and another brother, John of Gaunt, shares his ambition.

"That's enough for background. Now we'll make this castle come to life. Here we go."

Or rather, off I went, filling the castle with soldiers and the stables with horses as if I'd been present when Roger Mortimer came to Dover to take up residence and raise his flag on the central Keep.

Oh yes, here he was again—clear-eyed, bearded, broad-shouldered, born to leadership as I'd already pictured him: and now created by the king Constable of Dover and Warden of the Cinque Ports . . . Roger Mortimer, Earl of March, charged by the Black Prince to mastermind the invasion of France . . .

The story was gaining pace. "Horsemen thundering from the Palace Gate, carrying the Constable's orders to the seamen of the

Cinque Ports—north-east to Sandwich, westward to Rye and Hastings. Hurry, hurry, are you ready with the cross-channel transports for the men and the horses? The Black Prince due in Sandwich to take command . . . Mortimer in charge of the main invasion force, taking with him the ageing king . . .

"Down on the quayside, chandlers busy, ropes repairing, sails being tested . . .

"Within the castle men-at-arms assembling, fifteen hundred Kentish archers quartered by the North Barbican: smiths at the Armoury Tower checking Mortimer's steel gauntlets and new conical helmet: the saddlers and grooms at the Fitzwilliam Gate trying out the horses' harness: young Edmund Mortimer and a fellow pupil escaping from their priest-tutor to talk with an old soldier who was the boys' special friend within the garrison: and the Lady Philippa making daily intercession at St. Mary-in-Castro, praying for the success of the expedition . . .

"At last all is ready and the great invasion force embarks for France."

I paused for a moment, and the questions started. "Yes, Anderson, that's the Palace

Gate." "The smiths are on the other side, Brown, beside the Armoury Tower."

"The flag, sir, was it the same as the one Winston Churchill flew at Chartwell?"

"Where did Edmund and his friend live? Bit of luck getting off school to watch the armourers at work . . ."

It was time to make a move.

We scrambled into the minibus and, on the way back to school, stopped at Sandwich where we bought a round of ice cream cornets, consuming them at the quayside beside the ancient Barbican which still stands guard at the townward end of the bridge across the River Stour. At once, the questions began again.

"But, sir . . . you must tell us, sir, what happened to the expedition?"

"I was keeping that for school," I replied, "but I have to admit that the king's attempt to win the French crown was a dismal flop. Everything went wrong. First, a force of mercenaries already in France and commanded by young John of Gaunt got into difficulties and had to be rescued by the experienced Mortimer. Next, the Black Prince was late out of Sandwich. Then, when at last the English commanders assembled their forces and marched on Rheims where Edward III was to be crowned king of France, the French laid waste the countryside so that the English were deprived of food for their men and fodder for the horses. And finally, Roger Mortimer was killed on a foraging expedition into Burgundy." I was flattered by the boys' audible disappointment. "So they patched up a treaty of sorts," I continued, "which left the English in charge of south-west France, which they ruled from Bordeaux. (Yes, Anderson, that's where claret comes from)."

"And Mortimer, where's he buried?" (schoolboys take a strictly objective view of death).

"Oh, his body was brought back to Dover and then conveyed to a place called Wigmore on the borders of Wales. You can picture for yourselves the slow, sad journey, with people doffing their caps and crossing themselves as the cortège passed by—black horses hauling the carriage over the rough road, a posse of knights riding alongside wearing the blue and silver of the Mortimers, and behind the knights, Mortimer's widow on horseback accompanied by her son, Edmund, and his trusted friends, the old man-at-arms and the priest-tutor . . . it was a sad story."

My voice trailed away and we crowded back into the bus. But I told them that the expedition to France was only one chapter in Dover's history and even my story ended on a happier note since the Black Prince and the king took special care of Roger Mortimer's son. To a further questioner, I even confirmed that young Edmund was the same age as they were and that his tutor was the same age as I.

Well, at least part of the story was true, and it provided the class with some useful dates and a better knowledge of the shape of France. In due course it produced a set of essays which made surprisingly good reading. Most of the boys built up the battle scenes and the channel crossing— with fighting as gory as anything in the Iliad, and the Black Prince and Roger Mortimer no less heroic than Achilles and Ajax.

But there was one boy who took a different line. Daniel Berners-Levine stuck to Dover Castle after the expedition set sail, with Lady Philippa waiting with fear in her heart for news from France. He pictured her, I remember, talking with the young tutor in the Outer Baillie while her only son lay asleep in his room and a full moon shed its cold, eerie light on the battlements of the castle.

Harold Goldworthy was greatly impressed. "If Daniel produces something as good as that when the scholarship season comes round, I guarantee he'll win top place to Westminster."

It was the natural reaction of a schoolmaster. But later, as I recalled our day at the castle, I realised that the boy in the story was as real to me as the boys I was teaching: and that in Dover, as in Ockenham, Leeds and Oxford, I had been very close to young Edmund Mortimer's tutor, Nicholas Maidstone.

4

AT this time I still felt more at ease in Goldworthy's School than I did in my mother's Maidstone house: but an easier relationship had certainly developed between us since our motoring holiday to the Welsh border counties. So much so, that in the course of the holidays I told her more about my visits to Ockenham and Dover.

"It's hard to explain," I concluded, "but Nicholas has become more to me than an imaginary travelling companion. He's sort of taken shape."

"Well," she said, "I could hardly believe you created Nicholas on the spur of the moment, out of thin air. But why don't you take me to this village where you first discovered him?"

And so at the start of the spring term my mother drove me back to school via Ockenham. In order to look at the village and its neighbourhood, we reached the car park of the Wotton Arms a couple of hours before lunch. There was rain in the air, but it was warm for the time of year and we decided to take a walk along the public footpath which starts at the lodge gates of the Great House. This path leads across the park and so, past an oasthouse and a group of cottages, to the Dower House—a Georgian building which lies close to the Chartham road. We planned to return to the church and village by the main road.

To the left of us, the Great House silently surveyed the Mortimer-Wotton kingdom, its south elevation splendidly restored after the war damage, and an ancient moat protecting the formal rose garden in its immediate foreground. The house looked as strong and permanent as the land it overlooked.

My mother said, "The house must have changed its shape since young Nicholas and his master lived in these parts. Is it really true that the present owner traces direct descent from the Mortimers that your Nicholas served?"

"I really don't know," I replied. "It was only a junior branch of the Mortimer family that lived here in the early days—not the famous characters whose names you found in the Dictionary of National Biography. And the evidence in the church makes it clear that, during the reign of Henry VIII, the Wottons took over the place."

As we talked, we crossed an old stone bridge over the stream that flows down the valley into the lake, and so reached the main road.

It was there, at a point furthest from the village, that a burst of heavy rain sent us racing for cover to a bunch of evergreens by the roadside. We were getting what protection we could, when a car drew up beside us—a pre-war Rolls, bible-black, with high upright seats of a most forbidding dignity. At the wheel sat a good-looking, middle-aged man with fair hair, blue eyes and a military moustache: and beside him, a black Labrador looking straight ahead and apparently indifferent to all other road-users.

"Looks as if you could do with a lift," the driver said, leaning across the dog and opening the passenger door. "Can I take you as far as the village?"

My mother gratefully ran from the shelter of the trees but hesitated to enter the car as the Labrador made no move, until the driver heaved the animal over the back and into the rear seat.

"Sorry about Carla," he said to my mother, "the lazy old bitch is a little hard of hearing" and then, over his shoulder to me as I opened the rear door, "Don't worry about the dog: she's totally harmless, a softy like the rest of her breed."

We soon reached the Wotton Arms where mother's car was parked. As we thanked the driver he said, "Glad to be of help. I'm sure the publican will look after you. If you happen to be staying for a meal, I strongly recommend his wife's Canelloni."

With that, he completed a ponderous three-point turn in the car park and drove back at a dignified pace up the village street. We saw the Labrador jump back with surprising agility into the front seat beside her tweed jacketed master: and then man and dog, clearly a partnership of long standing, disappeared from view as the black Rolls wheeled into the Lodge gates at the far end of the village street.

It was my first meeting with Philip Mortimer-Wotton. But the family name stuck in my mind like the hit-song of a musical. At what point in history had the Mortimers joined with the Wottons? And how had the family managed to retain its grip on this small corner of England through all the changes of the last nine hundred years? What a perfect opening for investigation to a man with an interest in history and time on his hands.

After lunch—the Canelloni and a half-carafe of a dry Soave fully met the Major's recommendation—we were lingering over coffee when the name of Henry Yvele in the church guide attracted my attention.

"Yvele," I read aloud, pronouncing the name like our own surname, "this famous builder who is said to have been responsible for the fan-roofing in the church . . ." I stopped abruptly. "Didn't you tell me once, Mother, that father always claimed descent from a Kent yeoman's family? What's the betting that this Henry is one of our ancestors?" My mother looked at me in a curious way, part doubtful, part speculative.

"You've got a good memory," she said, "but I reckon that was one of your father's more imaginative theories. He never produced any evidence to support his assertions. Personally, I don't care a damn for heredity, anyway. In my view, each man born into this world has his individual value. If he happens to be born with a silver spoon in his mouth, the odds are he'll stick in his own rut like Major what's-his-name, and take the world for granted. But if he's born humble, he has an incentive to get clear of his starting-point. Either way, I could argue that ancestors are a handicap rather than a help." My mother seemed determined to dismiss father's theories once and for all.

The winter sun was emerging from the rain-washed sky as we walked up the village street and turned right to climb the hill to the church. As we entered by the south door I was again struck by the strength of the architecture and the beauty of the interior roofing. Even the priest's room, built over an extended south porch, added variety to the main building without disturbing its symmetry.

We made a leisurely inspection of the church and were on the point of leaving when my mother felt a bit foot-weary and asked me to go back to the pub and collect the car while she stayed in the church.

On my return, I was surprised to see her kneeling at the altar rail in the chancel. I could not remember a day when she had visited a church for any reason at all except as a holiday visitor, to inspect something that "rated a visit" in the guide book.

She cannot have heard me re-enter the church and I hesitated to disturb her. For a few minutes I sat in a pew at the west end of the nave, my eyes focused on the fan-vaulting of the transept. Was it possible that some ancestor of mine had planned and executed this roof of intricate, geometrical perfection?

The thought fascinated me. In the eerie light of a January afternoon I imagined a team of master-craftsmen working under Yvele's direction—contemporaries, without a doubt, of those great servants of the king, Roger and Edmund Mortimer and their priest-tutor, Nicholas Maidstone.

Nothing stirred in the place. Outside the sun must have been obscured by cloud, for the light no longer slanted across the church from the south transept window. Yet in the dim light I fancied I saw Nicholas celebrating the Mass at the altar. Had he come to this church, I wondered, after Roger Mortimer's death in that obscure skirmish in Burgundy in 1359? Or had he remained for a time beside Roger's brilliant son, Edmund, rising beside him in the royal service as learned clerks were wont to do in fourteenth-century England? Or had Wycliff's teaching at Oxford so infected him that he had made a diplomatic retreat from the Court to this obscure village? Even here, judging by the dates of his incumbency at St. Dunstan's, he must have lived through Wat Tyler's Peasants' Revolt. He might even have marched on London with the Men of Kent and the Kentish Men . . .

The silence in the church was broken by the sound of my mother's footsteps. I saw her returning down the flagged, uncarpeted central aisle, her steps slower, more hesitant than the brisk pace to which my ears were attuned.

"Oh, there you are," she said. "No trouble with the car, I hope?"

"None at all," I replied. "It's waiting at the gate into the churchyard. But I didn't like to disturb you."

She looked up at me and I noticed that her eyes were filled with tears. I don't think I'd ever seen her showing emotion like this. Somehow, our relationship had recently been more akin to the tolerant friendship of two lodgers who chance to live in the same house. Now, for the first time in my adult life, I felt moved to put my arm round her. I steered her quietly out of the church, past the line of ancient yews to the lychgate and the car. She seemed very tired, as if suddenly conscious of her age. No words passed between us.

I settled her in the passenger seat and drove towards Canterbury. But as we emerged from the city on the Whitstable road, she broke the silence and said in a strained voice,

"Richard, there's something I have to tell you, something you don't know, something you ought to know, something your father knew . . ."

I turned the car into a parking area just off the road. The rain had started again.

"What is it, Mother?" I said. "Is it something you saw in the church?"

She grasped my hands with a sort of feverish strength. "No, Richard, it started back at the pub when you asked about your father's connection with Henry Yvele. And then, when I looked up to the chancel roof in the church, I knew I could no longer keep silent. You see, you are not your father's son . . . you are not my son . . ."

In the confined space of the car, with the raindrops splashing on the car bonnet and the January wind whistling through the bare trees outside, I felt completely cut off from the world I knew. I was alone with the woman I'd never called anything but Mother. Was I learning at last why I'd never felt or experienced the affection that other sons must know?

"Go on," I said, "go on."

"I loved your father," she continued. "You must understand this. Tom was thirty-five years old—the same age as I was —when we first met. Sometimes he used to have fits of depression, stemming from his terrible memories of trench warfare. But I didn't marry him out of pity. No, I loved him because he was fine and brave, and I wanted—oh, so badly—to give him a baby. But it didn't work out."

It seemed also, from what she said, that her father was always somewhere in the background, anxious for an heir to the family business he was so proud of. At any rate, when they were sure they could not have a child of their own, Tom and she applied to an adoption society and, with old Brooke's full approval, I was duly received into the family and christened in the family name.

She began to cry as she remembered the sequence of events. "For a time everything went well. But then Tom died, and my father died . . . and the business had to be sold . . . and so, what I should have told you as a child was never told. Never, that is, until I was alone in the church this afternoon and the truth seemed to be forced out of me. I've been so silly, Richard . . . but it seemed right at the time. Please, please forgive me."

It was a strange situation. I'd never bothered about my ancestry. Only a chance remark of mine had caused my mother to stammer out the truth that I was an adopted child. But was it I? Or was some other force at work? I remember I brushed aside her anxiety, trying to alleviate her grief.

"Don't distress yourself, it doesn't alter anything. We're just the same as we were yesterday. We need each other. You said yourself that ancestors can be a problem."

We drove the last remaining miles to the school. I showed her my digs, in a house away from the main school buildings. We unpacked my things and we brewed up some tea and I asked her if she would not like to stay the night. But no. She had no fear about driving back to Maidstone. And so I waved goodbye to my adopted mother, watching the headlamps of her little car as they pierced the blackness of the dark road home.

5

I RETURNED to the house on the far side of the playing fields in a mood compounded of self-pity, resentment and loneliness. Every link with the past, a lie. My identity, a blank. My romantic connection with Henry Yvele, sheer fantasy. And yet, a confused feeling deep inside me that I had some personal link with this village in East Kent. Past, present, future? Who was I, then? Where the hell did I go from here? And after all these years of illusion, with whom could I share my preoccupations?

I was still sitting hunched in a rickety armchair when Keith Figgis, who shares the accommodation with me, barged in. He was at his most intolerable.

"Hullo, you old bastard," he greeted me, absurdly unconscious of the truth of the appellation. "Back first, eh? So what's new? Nothing to do, I suppose, until the little perishers return tomorrow from their luxury homes? Well, what do you say to a couple of hours, kicking the gong around the town?"

I told him to kick his bloody gong anywhere he liked: I wasn't interested. But Keith is one of those persistent chaps who are hard to shake off. He suffers from too much money: and because he enjoys his leisure, he under-uses his abilities which are not inconsiderable. Privately I admit I envy him his good looks, his self-confidence and his ease in company, even his skill as an all-round athlete. But provided I take him in small quantities, I manage to remain on reasonably good terms with him.

On this occasion he had a plan, he said. A Dickens evening, no less.

"Look, Richard, this will interest you. I've picked up a book in a second-hand shop in the Charing Cross Road. All about the drinking habits of Mr. C. Dickens. A convivial bloke, our Charles: and this book gives a fascinating insight into Victorian drinking habits. Tonight, we put the recipes to the test in Broadstairs where the great man used to stay in order to recharge his batteries. Come on. I can't go drinking alone, and we shall be well away from Ma

Goldworthy's spy network. I'll do the driving. What do you say?"

In the end, I gave up arguing: and we raced into Broadstairs in Keith's little MG. We parked and locked the car beside the old harbour where we pictured the novelist enjoying the ozone before it was poisoned by petrol fumes. Then we moved on foot to a smart-looking pub.

Keith consulted his little book, and addressed himself to the astonished barmaid.

"Dog's Nose for two," he ordered confidently, "as provided, my love, at the Magpie and Stump in Clare Market." For the girl's further enlightenment he stated the ingredients in detail: one pint warmed Guinness, a nip of gin, a tablespoon of brown sugar and a pinch of nutmeg. "No nutmeg? Well, we'll have to make do without the final ingredient." Keith was in his element.

"Nothing like Guinness for a good foundation, Richard. These Victorians knew what was good for them." We sipped the mixture slowly. "Next, we'll have a Black Velvet—Guinness and Champagne." Keith continued to study his newly purchased book. "I doubt if we can get together Micawber's Gin Punch—too sweet anyway with honey, sugar and madeira added to the gin. And Smoking Bishop, though excellent, takes an age to prepare. But what about Pursers' Purge—one brandy, two dry gin, a dash of Angostura with ice and lemon juice? That sounds a nice thirst-quencher to finish with."

We moved from one pub to another, swallowing an extraordinary variety of concoctions known to Mr. Pickwick and Dick Swiveller, the red-nosed Stiggins, and other Dickens drinking men. I believe I got as far as the Pursers' Purge before I opted out. I could not swallow another drop, and left Keith in favour of fresh air. Once outside the pub, I found myself wandering into the town without any clear sense of purpose or direction.

It was then that I knew I was hopelessly drunk. Whether I saw Keith again was a matter of no importance. How I found my way back to the school was irrelevant. From time to time I imitated an Army sergeant shouting at a squad of new recruits, "All out of step except one little bastard—you there, you." The old parade ground joke seemed to dispel my earlier mood.

Soon I was completely lost. My steps must have taken me up the hill from the harbour and the town centre, for I was proceeding happily down a row of villa-type houses when the Law, in the shape of a large bearded policeman, caught up with me.

"Celebratin', are yer?" The voice was heavily sarcastic. "Walkin' the way you do, you'll pitch yourself under a car: and yer mother wouldn't like that, would she? Better get 'ome quick—or we'll 'ave to pull you in, if only to stop you wakin' the neighbours. Now where *do* you live?"

At the close of this ponderous monologue, the huge man shifted slightly and I caught sight of the road sign: Cherry Tree Close. Something clicked in my addled mind. Number 37—that was where Rosie Ashcroft, the music mistress, lived with her two young sons. A good sort, Rosie. One of the best friends I'd got on Goldworthy's staff. A war widow in her thirties. A splendidly sensible person as well as a first-class pianist. Good, reliable Rosie, she'd know how to cope.

"Officer," I said, "have no fear. I'm nearly home—Number 37, to be exact. Radio silence will be observed. My apologies for bothering you."

He must have decided I was harmless, for he put away his little book and I walked unsteadily down the road with the man's eyes boring into my back. To my relief a light was shining from the front room at Number 37 and Rosie Ashcroft opened the door.

"Good God, Richard," she said. "What on earth have you been up to? You're a bit late calling, aren't you?"

"Shush," I said, "I've got a policeman trailing me. Just let me in and I'll explain everything."

"So that's how it is," she replied. "Well, for Pete's sake, come in quickly and try not to knock anything over or you'll wake the boys."

She piloted me to a settee, and bustled off to the kitchen. A few minutes later she was back with a pot of tea and a couple of aspirin. "Now," she said, pouring out the tea, "what on earth causes you to be drinking yourself silly in Broadstairs? I know it's not my concern: but you're some way off your usual stamping ground, aren't you?"

For a time I remained silent, sipping the tea, and looking round the trim sitting-room, unexceptional except for a baby grand piano at one end of the room. The keyboard was open and it looked as if Rosie had been playing. She must have followed my gaze, for she said,

"I don't know how many times I've thanked God for that piano. Since John was killed, it's really my only companion, once the lights are out in the boys' bedrooms."

There was no self-pity in her manner. Yet something in the tone of her voice—part bravery, part acceptance, I suppose—pulled my mind back to my mother.

Instead of talking about Keith Figgis and the ghastly potations of our Dickens evening, I told Rosie of my mother's confession earlier in the day. It was only the following morning I discovered the extent to which I had burbled on. For the rest of that evening, Rosie was strictly practical.

"Shoes off, Richard," I remember her saying, "coat off. Undo your tie. Here's a rug. Put your feet up. That's right. I'll run

74

you back to school tomorrow. If the boys ask questions in the morning, we'll say Keith's car broke down after the garage was closed. Right? Now I'll play something to send you off to sleep." She crossed the room to the piano and struck the first soft chords of Schubert's G major Sonata.

The last I heard of it was the close of the slow movement. Next morning I woke to find a small table beside the settee, and on it a glass of water and a packet of Alka-Seltzer.

By the time I had sorted myself out, Rosie was already up and busy with breakfast. With her unfussy efficiency she had fixed for the boys to spend the morning with friends. "Swimming and lunch" I gathered from the elder boy who seemed to take my presence for granted, and enlightened me on a forthcoming swimming test which might win him a gold badge which would have to be sewn onto his bathing trunks. Doubtless Rosie would be happy to oblige.

By ten o'clock the boys had disappeared, and Rosie was driving me back to the school at Cliff's End. I began to blurt out a mixture of apologies for my behaviour and thanks for her kindness, but she shut me up.

"Forget it," she said, "these things happen—especially with people like Keith. But tell me, have you any idea what you were talking about last night?"

"Well, not exactly," I replied. "But I think I may have told you I was an adopted child. My so-called mother only told me yesterday—and it came as a bit of a shock, I can tell you."

"Poor old Richard," she said, "but what about your mother? Of course, she should have told you the truth long ago. Breaking her long silence must have been terribly difficult for her: and she is the one who is going to suffer most. You can adjust to change, but her conscience will be loaded with something she'll find it hard to forget."

She looked at me for a moment, wondering whether to say more. Then she continued, her mind made up.

"But, Richard, you also rambled on about a village called Ockenham and a priest you referred to as Nicholas. You were very odd, as if you reckoned this priest had also heard your mother's confession. An old church came into the story, too. Then you suddenly switched into history, naming that Shakespearean grey-beard, John of Gaunt, as villain extraordinary. You really were in one hell of an alcoholic muddle."

I came to a sudden decision. "Look," I said, "it's a long story. There's no hurry to get back to the school. If you can spare the time, why not drive down to the cliff car park and I'll try to explain?"

Rosie was a good listener. We stared out of the car across the grey waters of Sandwich Bay and I told her all. I explained how I had first been confronted in Ockenham churchyard by this terrified priest crying vengeance on John of Gaunt for the murder of young Mortimer. Then I explained how I had tried to amuse my mother by inventing a story about this fourteenth-century priest, only to find myself involved with him and a class of Wycliff students in Oxford.

"OK, OK," she laughed. "And then you met your priest and a gaggle of Mortimers at Dover Castle. Daniel Berners-Levine told us about it last term. Pretty riveting stuff; I gather. Said you got 'quite carried away'. I'd say Mr. Richard Eveleigh's stock went up a lot with the boys after that performance."

I began to laugh, too. Chatting with this young widow, I realised how silly the story sounded . . . silly until I became aware of Rosie's grey eyes staring at me—and not at the sand dunes and the sea in front of us.

"I don't think it's silly," she said. "Johnnie used to have similar moments during the war and he used to tell me about them. They didn't mean anything to me until after the mission from which he didn't return. But since he and his bomber ditched in the North Sea, I've often wondered whether these odd pictures from the past didn't presage the future . . . he had a New England pitch, I remember . . . witches burning and sailors drowning and so on." She jerked herself back to the present. "If you believe that life stretches into the future beyond death, doesn't it also imply a link with the years before you were born? Some people see and feel these things more clearly than others. That's all."

She pressed the starter and drove me back to the school. "See you tomorrow," she said, "back at the Goldworthy treadmill. But don't be surprised if your fourteenth-century characters go on pestering you until you get the message. They don't sound to me like 'live and let live' types. I wouldn't mind betting a Broadstairs dinner that you change your job before the year is out."

6

SUMMER TERM at Goldworthy's started well. The May weather that year was warm and sunny, and in June Daniel Berners-Levine duly landed the top scholarship at Westminster. The boy was an odds-on winner in any case, but I was secretly gratified when Goldworthy and the boy's parents gave me some credit for Daniel's success.

Among the parents at this particular school the father, Monty Berners-Levine, was a lonely and somewhat unusual character. Born the poor son of a Jewish tailor in Whitechapel, he had come into money the hard way. I was to know him far better in the years ahead. But even at my first meeting at a celebratory lunch to which he and his wife invited me, I sensed the driving force behind his rise to riches —the quick, intuitive mind; the application, the willingness to take risks in the post-war property boom, culminating in this determination to ensure that his two boys enjoyed the sort of private education which he and his wife had missed. I was also amused by his sheer enjoyment of the five-star luxury his wealth made possible: and his indifference, even contempt, for the other parents who would, to his certain knowledge, consider him "vulgar", "osten-tatious" and "anyway, what did he do in the war?"

At that first meeting, he took me after lunch for a walk in the hotel gardens and, puffing at a Corona-size Havana, started to talk about his second boy who had just reached the school.

"I'll be grateful," he said, "if you can keep an eye on young Paul. He lacks the brain-power which makes school life comparatively easy for Daniel. He is wrapped up in music and we even considered a specifically musical education, but as he is small for his age and rather unsure of himself, we thought it better to send him to this school where Daniel has made his mark. You see what I mean?"

I assured him that he need have no fear for the boy. Any sign of bullying, I told him, would be dealt with very firmly by the headmaster, and Mrs. Ashcroft would certainly encourage his musical gifts. Monty and his wife seemed greatly relieved, and I put the matter out of my mind.

A week later, however, my new and higher standing with Goldworthy was shaken by events which started with an entirely ridiculous incident in the course of the school cricket match against the parents. In this annual event, very dear to the head-master's heart, a parents' eleven plays a mixed team of masters and boys. The idea is to generate a happy family spirit between staff, parents and boys: but it doesn't always work this way, in spite of the care with which the headmaster lays his plans. A few days before the great day, I received my orders from Harold Goldworthy.

"A word with you, Richard," he said. "We shall need you in the side because Figgis has been asked to play for the County second eleven; and I may have to give you a bowl if the parents are short of runs." The headmaster didn't mean to be offensive—it was just his idea of a joke. "But as it's the first time you've been included in the show, let me remind you that Lord Speymore should not be dismissed until his score reaches double figures. He's an appalling batsman, but he insists on playing as long as his brood of boys is with us. We don't want to mess up a happy relationship, understand?"

I thought no more of this astonishing instruction. These private schools have their own *mores*. Who am I to question them?

But you can guess the rest. The parents batted badly and the headmaster handed me the ball just as Speymore arrived at the wicket. My first ball was a wide—excellent. My second trickled down the pitch to his Lordship who blocked the ball with exaggerated care, contemptuously picked up the ball and returned it to me—excellent, though a little humiliating. "Pitch it up, Richard, for heaven's sake," hissed the headmaster from mid-off. I did so—a juicy half-volley which should have been struck out of the ground. But you never can tell. Speymore hit the ball hard enough, but straight at me head-high. In sheer self-defence, I put up my hands and the ball stuck: Lord Speymore caught and bowled Eveleigh without scoring. The headmaster, like the great queen, was not amused. I think he believed, as did the two other masters in the side, that I had fixed Speymore on purpose.

The noble Lord's dismissal could be classified as a minor incident. Not so the subsequent row which developed with the new school matron. Edna Clarke was, as I have briefly mentioned, a fifty-year-old spinster, well qualified for the job by her considerable previous experience. But she had a peculiar aptitude for spying, and the staff had good reason for disliking her. She knew when you returned late from a party. She knew which pubs you visited. She put sinister interpretations on innocent escapades: and she was liable to transmit her thoughts and suspicions to Ma Goldworthy. In my particular case, the trouble concerned the young woman who had just been appointed as assistant matron.

Diana Murray, who took up her post in the summer term, was young, only just out of school, and very pretty. She had dark hair with a natural wave, a warm, clear skin and eyes that seemed to reflect the sunshine.

To nobody's surprise Keith Figgis made

the first pass at her, took her out in his MG and managed to be on hand whenever Diana was free. To bait me, he would return to the digs and analyse the course of his romance. "Lovely, firm young body," he would say; "innocent of course, but all in good time, eh? . . . not quite the war service experience of Mary Winter, old boy . . . but we'll see . . . we'll see." His crack about Mary Winter was particularly offensive, as though she had seduced me with his prior knowledge. The truth is that Keith was totally crude in his assessment of women. I'd heard it all before—but generally his observations concerned a pick-up in Margate or some sophisticated "date" in London. Let him include Mary in his generalisations if he wanted to. She'd know how to put him in his place. But with Diana it was different. Somehow I kept my temper and refused to be drawn, waiting for the weekend of the parents' match when Keith would be at the other end of the county. As we came off the field, I saw Diana sitting with a group of boys near the pavilion. I joined her, pretending to myself that I wanted to keep clear of the headmaster and any snide remarks about my bowling.

She looked up as I approached. "In trouble with the management, Richard?" she said with a shy smile. "For my part, I thought his Lordship's dismissal was the highlight of an otherwise tedious afternoon, but I can imagine you might want to avoid the crowd for an hour or two."

When I said, a little testily, that I had no means of escape like a low-slung MG, she asked what was wrong with the local bus service. And so it came about that on that same evening Diana and I travelled by public transport to the little Cinque Port town of Sandwich. We walked by the quay and along the riverbank. Then we ordered a snack at the Admiral Crispin before catching the last bus back to Cliff's End. I can only remember that the four hours passed far too quickly, and we were back at the school much too soon. But at least I had time to discover that in Diana's view Keith Figgis need never cross her sights again. She didn't like his style one little bit.

"Thinks he's irresistible," she told me, her eyes reflecting her anger. "Pawing every girl he meets as if an MG gives him some special licence . . . disgusting . . . I've told him to stick to cricket: and as you share digs with the man, you may as well know how I feel."

I returned to my room in a state of absurd elation. It was only at our next meeting that Diana told me of her row with Aunt Edna for being home after midnight. For the rest of the term, Diana and I kept each other company. Keith, without any show of ill-feeling, gave up the race, contenting himself with a few snide remarks about baby-killing and reminding me that I was seven years older than Diana. But she must have delivered a knock-out punch, for he never tried to get into the act again.

In the week following our bus trip, Diana and I combined to hire a car in the village. And this acquisition led thereafter to sea bathing excursions, picnics on the cliffs above Dover, an occasional visit to the Marlowe Theatre at Canterbury and snack meals in an assortment of excellent local pubs. I thought to cast myself in the role of a gallant protector against the abominable Figgis. But I quickly learnt that the eighteen-year-old Diana needed no such protection. Really we were equal in everything but age. As a doctor's daughter and with a home in the Surrey stockbroker belt, she probably had more experience of the outside world than I. But in one respect our backgrounds were similar. Like me, she had signed on at Goldworthy's for the sole purpose of getting away from a difficult home situation. Mrs. Murray, if her daughter's estimate was correct, was completely tied up with Conservative Party coffee mornings and bridge evenings, with gin-and-tonics to fuel the engines after sunset. Diana was not prepared to conform either to her mother's lifestyle or her politics.

Inevitably, Aunt Edna's displeasure was directed at me as well as Diana: and I was greatly irritated when the headmaster warned me to watch my step as Miss Clarke felt very responsible for a girl of Diana's age. Not that it made any difference to our behaviour. We made no effort to appease Aunt Edna and, indeed, Diana decided to resign her job at the end of the term in the hope of finding a more congenial boss.

Our meetings were interrupted, however, not by the innuendos of the vindictive Miss Clarke, but by news that my mother had suffered a severe stroke which had affected her speech and paralysed her right side. It was totally unexpected, for she was physically strong and there had been no warning symptoms.

The headmaster, who received the news by phone from mother's neighbour, was most sympathetic and gave me immediate leave of absence: but on reaching the hospital at Maidstone I found I could do very little to help.

I was dreadfully shocked by my mother's appearance—as much by the glazed look in her eyes and the lack of interest in the world around her, as by her inability to communicate. I gained that curious impression, which I have since experienced in hospital visiting, of a person who had decided to make no effort to recover or to hold on to life. It was the more unusual because I had always thought of my mother as a most determined woman. But the neighbour who had a key to mother's house confirmed my opinion. She promised to make regular visits to the hospital and keep in touch with me by phone. Yet I think I was still more worried by my abject failure to express my thanks to this dying woman for the care and love she had given during her active life to the child she had adopted. Now it was too late. Only now, as I left my mother's bedside, did I know in my heart the useless remorse of a man who has for too long left gratitude unspoken.

Returning to the school in my mother's car, I was suddenly gripped by the belief that my mother's stroke was linked with her confession on the road from Ockenham. Had Rosie Ashcroft been right in thinking that her conscience would be harder to live with than my newly acquired knowledge of my beginnings? Was I, in one sense, responsible? And how could I make amends?

My questions were never answered. Ten days later, my mother died in hospital after suffering a further stroke. I was assured that nobody could have helped her, but something impelled me to return to Maidstone by way of Ockenham. In penitence I entered the old church of St. Dunstan, walked up the central aisle to the chancel rail and knelt where my mother had knelt some six months previously. The silence in the church was absolute. I formulated no prayer. I made no confession, nor consciously asked for forgiveness. Any thoughts I may have had for commending the dead woman's soul to a merciful God were unspoken. My ears were alert but they heard nothing.

I do not know how long I remained by the steps of the altar. Yet I am sure of one thing: as I left the church, the little priest was walking beside me. Though I can put no words in his mouth, his message to me was crystal clear. "Get out into the wider world, Richard. The enclosed order of a private school is not for you. I, too, escaped and I, too, was an illegitimate child."

I was almost light-hearted as I drove the rest of the way to Maidstone. I'd have to give Rosie Ashcroft dinner in Broadstairs— we'd go, no doubt to Marquesi's admirable *ristorante*. And I'd need to give Gold-worthy notice which meant one more term at the school. And then? I had no answer, except that I was free to choose . . . free to choose. Mother's death meant for me a new beginning.

7

IT was time, I was sure, to leave the school at Cliff's End. Rosie's odd prediction, Diana Murray's departure, my mother's death and my consequent sense of freedom—even the promptings of the Ockenham priest—everything conspired to press me into making a break. I went so far as to warn Harold Goldworthy in writing that I would wish to leave the school at Christmas.

But I don't exactly make things happen, if you know what I mean, and my decision was complicated by a letter from Harold Goldworthy which crossed with mine and followed closely on an earlier letter of sympathy—one of several I had received from members of the staff and, rather touchingly, from some of the boys.

The headmaster's second letter read as follows:

Dear Richard,
     I hesitate to intrude on your private

sorrow: but I have been wondering how you are placed for the summer vacation. My wife and I have reason to know that in the face of sudden and unexpected bereavement a man's life may slip into a hopeless vacuum unless he quickly finds something positive to do.

With this thought in mind, I am writing to you about a holiday tutoring job on which my advice has recently been sought.

Piers Bovill is a somewhat lonely twelve-year-old who has lost much of his schooling through illness. His sisters, who are much older than he is, have a very full social life in London while his parents, Lord and Lady Eglemont, are out of the country until mid-September. They seem anxious about the boy's prospects for the Eton entrance exam next year.

I would not be greatly surprised to learn that the boy is more in need of companionship than instruction.

To my mind you could fit the job specification very well: and it would mean that during the next five weeks you will be assured of reasonable independence, as well as a decent salary and free lodging at the Eglemonts' place near Ashford.

Lord Eglemont's agent, Captain Dickinson, knows I have approached you. A quick "Yes" or "No" would be greatly appreciated. The address is Monteagle House, Ashford (Tel. Ashford 242). Do let me know what you decide.

Sincerely, as ever,
Harold Goldworthy

Shrewd old headmaster! I accepted his diagnosis of my situation without question, though I suspected that his real motive was to retain my services. Two days later, after telephone calls to him and Lord Eglemont's agent, I presented myself at Monteagle House—a vast eighteenth-century mansion set in its own acres and reached by a mile-long winding track through gently undulating pasture land. Even as I chugged up the drive in mother's old Morris, I saw from the tarmac road surface and neat fencing that somebody was exercising excellent control over the estate and the farming. The agent, Hugh Dickinson, greeted me at the front door. He and his wife, Margaret, lived in one wing of the house: and it was evident that between them they carried a considerable responsibility for the running of the house as well as the estate. It was clear, too, that I had entered a world of which I had no previous experience.

There was no sign of the boy, Piers, but Simmonds, the butler, showed me to my room which was adjacent to where the boy slept, and arranged for my luggage to be brought upstairs and my car to be garaged in the stables.

I think that Piers' absence had been specially contrived, for during tea which was served in a smallish room off the entrance hall, Hugh and Margaret Dickinson provided me with some background information about my charge. From them I gathered that the boy did not fit easily into the County land-owning world which the Dickinsons as well as the boy's family graced so naturally.

Hugh Dickinson, lately with the 12th Lancers, summed up the boy's situation with understanding and not without affection.

"Sisters in London, parents constantly overseas, doesn't like horses, prefers bird-watching to cricket, unhappy in the traditional schooling to which he is committed—in short, a square peg in a round hole. Hardly surprising if he's a bit of a loner. May be hard for him to find his way in life."

The Dickinsons, who had no children of their own, were thoroughly concerned about the boy for whom they felt a quasi-parental responsibility. "Apart from us, his best friends are people who are always here at Monteagle—Simmonds, the cook, the gardener, some of the farm hands and so on."

Piers proved every bit as difficult as the Dickinsons had hinted. He was below average in height, not very strong: and when we first met, uncommunicative about his interests, and resentful of my presence at Monteagle House.

The first few days were hard going, but I was soon able to confirm to the Dickinsons that Piers was not in the least "backward" in the educational sense—just bored stiff with the teaching of a school which seemed solely concerned with exam results. A few mathematical tests and some reading followed by a few essays proved that he could waltz through the Common Entrance. I suspected that his IQ was higher than the school realised. With more imaginative teaching he might have picked up a scholarship, though not perhaps at Eton.

With the Dickinsons' agreement, I stopped all formal lessons and spent the long summer days with Piers on local walks and expeditions into the surrounding countryside—sometimes in my car, sometimes on bicycles. Gradually the boy began to unwind. I remember I won his special gratitude by cancelling three junior cricket games to which his silly mother had committed him.

"So good for Piers to mix with other boys his own age." The boy imitated the parental voice to perfection, and added, "Richard, tell me honestly, have you ever tried mixing with people your own age when you are told to field all day at long leg, and regularly make a duck if by some stray chance you're allowed to bat?"

I told him I had endured the same purgatory and made him laugh over my performance in the parents' match at Cliff's End. From that moment we were friends. For the rest of my stay at Monteagle, cricketers were dismissed as "flannelled fools".

On the other hand, I discovered that Piers was keenly interested in his family history. One day he told me of its origins at Aigle in Normandy, of its arrival in England with the Conqueror and settlement in this marvellous farming area of Kent.

"Not many chaps still around with that sort of history," I said casually. "Ever met the Mortimer-Wottons over at Ockenham?" The boy thought his father and mother knew Philip Mortimer-Wotton reasonably well, but why was I asking? So I told him about my visit to Ockenham which had sparked my interest in fourteenth-century England.

"Wat Tyler, and all that?" he said. "Found a book about him in father's library last holidays . . . Oman's *Peasant Revolt*. Bit dull, really: but Hugh Dickinson brought the show to life for me . . . he's very interested in local history, you know. Told me Wat Tyler was a demobbed soldier who hadn't been paid. Found the farm workers round here were pretty angry, too: so he persuaded them to join him and march to London to put their complaints before the new King, Richard the Second. According to Hugh, the peasant army moved from Canterbury to Blackheath faster than any march organised by the Black Prince against the French. Terrific, wasn't it? Took the government by surprise. At Maidstone they were joined by a mad priest who made them sing as they marched."

"Some people," I added, "still remember one of John Ball's old rhymes and ask the same question:

When Adam delved and Eve span,
Who was then the gentleman?"

Piers looked at me in surprised delight. "You know that one too, Richard? When I quoted it to father one day, he said he didn't want any damned communism round here. Got quite stuffy about it." Piers laughed. "Tell you what . . . we'll ask Hugh to let us make an expedition to London . . . follow the Peasant Army all the way to London and blow up the Savoy."

Young Piers seemed to link John of

Gaunt's luxury home with its five-star twentieth-century counterpart, for the association of ideas set him off on a new tack. "Might take in a theatre or a concert and stay the night at my sister's flat. Come on, Richard. What about it?"

The trip proved the highlight of Piers Bovill's summer holiday. In addition to a Variety Show at the Palladium, it included a quick look at the Archbishop's Palace beside the Medway at Maidstone, where Wat Tyler's army broke into the prison to release John Ball: thence to Blackheath where we lunched at a Transport Café near the very spot where the Men of Kent and Kentish Men had once pitched their camp prior to their descent on London: and finally we drove past the site of the Marshalsea prison and across London Bridge to the Tower where the young King and his advisers had taken refuge.

"And you're telling me, Richard, that the King was only eighteen years old? Gosh, he must have been terrified, seeing the fires spreading along the South Bank and hearing that the mob had destroyed his famous uncle's palace! But King Richard kept his nerve, didn't he?"

"Yes," I agreed, "he kept his nerve. Richard of Bordeaux was as brave as his father, the Black Prince. But he wasn't strong enough to keep the promises he made to the insurgents. His uncle, John of Gaunt, saw to that. More's the pity."

My voice must have betrayed my partisanship, for Piers looked at me and said, "You know, I rather like you, Richard. You sort of think like I do."

Our excursion into history ended when we reached the flat off St. James's, where Henrietta, one of the two Eglemont sisters, was in residence. She was fair haired, strikingly beautiful, and in her expensive clothes she would show up well at any society gathering. But she appeared to have no interest in her young brother's life or activities: and she could not conceal her boredom at working in a boutique off Bond Street in August while her sister was living it up at St. Tropez. Within a few hours, she inspired in me a total revulsion against her way of life. Not because she was rich, but because she wasted time and money on such a futile existence. Piers' interests were light-years away from his sisters' sophisticated world. I understood now why he was so desperately lonely.

On our return to Monteagle, the Dickinsons were genuinely interested to hear Piers' account of the trip to London—a fine medley of history and Flanagan and Allan.

"You've put new heart into him," they told me later. "He's got a new enthusiasm, a new light in his eye. What's the recipe? What's your honest opinion about him?"

I was coming to the end of my stay and decided to speak my mind.

"Piers is a fascinating lad," I told them. "Endowed with charm and brains. Your problem is his family. If Lord and Lady Eglemont want the boy to enjoy life and play his part at Monteagle, they must stop trying to type him. Otherwise they will have a bloody-minded rebel on their hands. I would suggest they stop thinking in terms of Eton. Go for some other school where his artistic instincts can be developed without being throttled by family or aristocratic tradition. Then, in due course, you may find yourself training him as your successor. I suspect he already understands the countrymen round here better than the other members of his family."

On my last morning at Monteagle Piers brought his early morning tea into my bedroom as he had done for the last three weeks; he looked so forlorn sitting in his pyjamas on the end of my bed. There were no plans to be made for the day except my departure. I saw the boy was very close to tears. Better be brisk, I thought, and get away early after breakfast. He insisted on accompanying me to the end of the long drive.

"We'll keep in touch," I said as we parted. "You have my address. Write if you want to: and don't worry. Hugh and Margaret Dickinson will see things right for you, and they won't let you down."

Piers jumped out. In the car's mirror I saw him greeted by an old lady in one of the cottages on the edge of the estate. He would be less lonely with her, I thought, than in the big house.

A week later, after sorting out my mother's affairs with our Maidstone solicitors, I returned to Cliff's End to find a "private and confidential" letter awaiting my arrival. It came from Monty Berners-Levine and asked me to keep a special eye on his second son, Paul. Evidently the old man and his wife were about to set sail on some luxury cruise to the West Indies so that Paul would not get home on either of the two "exeats" the boys were allowed each term.

Caught again, I thought to myself. First the Hon. Piers Bovill, and now Paul Berners-Levine. A couple of undersized schoolboys. Both nervous. Both a little lonely in their school surroundings. Both artistic and—in Paul's case—endowed with genuine musical talent. But there the similarity ended. Piers, with his grey eyes and fair hair, betraying his nervousness with a rather attractive stutter. Paul, with black hair and white cheeks, confident in speech and notable for those deep yet lively brown eyes which one sees in so many Jewish musicians. And their school background was fundamentally different too. Paul's parents were sending their child into territory they had never explored. The Eglemonts were trying to keep theirs within the confines of a class in society they had never left.

So, on the Sunday of the first "exeat" weekend I found myself committed to a day's outing with Paul Berners-Levine. To give ourselves an objective we drove to Ockenham, and walked where my mother and I had walked at the start of the year. In the park a herd of Guernseys was grazing: and their glowing colour was reflected in the autumn beauty of oak and beech. Beyond the park, the ground was ploughed and ready for sowing. Paul's eyes absorbed a sight which he would never see in Clapham SW. We took a quick look in the church after morning service before lunching at the Wotton Arms: and I found myself rather enjoying my "in loco parentis" status. I even experienced a curious feeling that I was on my home ground. Knowing Paul's interest in music, we slipped into Evensong in Canterbury Cathedral, and were back at the school just about the time the other boys were returning from their home weekends.

Paul was not exactly communicative, though I gained a fairly clear impression of his holiday existence—indulgent parents and the big house in Clapham which was the Berners-Levine home as well as the headquarters of Berninko Ltd., the property company from which the family derived its money. Later that week Rosie

Ashcroft assured me that the boy had loved his day out and had, in particular, expanded to her about the beauty of the singing in the Cathedral.

Music was going to be integral to this boy's life: and, as the term proceeded, I allowed him in his free time to use a new record player which I had installed in our digs. Rosie Ashcroft lent me records from time to time, and others among Rosie's pupils began to attend these sessions: there was nothing private about them. The headmaster approved. Gradually young Berners-Levine began to make friends with other boys who shared his musical interests.

But there was a problem. Young Paul began to look up to me with something akin to a puppy's devotion. He must also have written to his parents about my care for him, for one day I was embarrassed to receive a complete set of the Klemperer recordings of the Beethoven symphonies with an effusive note of thanks from Mrs. Berners-Levine.

At a private school nothing is hidden. Inevitably Edna Clarke, who had never forgiven me for my alleged part in Diana

Murray's departure in the summer, began to talk. She thought it "rather unhealthy", to use her own calculated understatement, for Paul Berners-Levine to be so much in my company, especially at weekends. Fortunately I heard of Aunt Edna's innuendos from Rosie Ashcroft before they reached the headmaster's ears. I thanked Rosie for the information, burst into the matron's sitting room and completely lost my temper. If she really thought in her nasty mind that I was a practising homosexual with designs on young Berners-Levine, why not come out with it straight? The old bitch blushed to the roots of her greying hair, told me she had never been so insulted in her life and would make an immediate complaint about my conduct to Mr. Goldworthy.

"No point in it," I replied. "I told the headmaster before the start of the term that I might wish to leave at Christmas. I shall now make my resignation official. I shall tell him that though I have enjoyed my time at the school, I am not prepared to spend another term in the same establishment as Edna Clarke. He can draw his own conclusions but, for the future, I would commend to you the motto of the three wise monkeys: 'Hear no evil, speak no evil, think no evil'."

I turned my back on the woman without waiting for her reply, slammed the door and cooled off in the school playing fields before handing my resignation to Harold Goldworthy.

On the last Saturday of term I carried out my final and very pleasant duty at Cliff's End. I kept my promise to Rosie Ashcroft and gave her a superb Italian meal at Marquesi's in Broadstairs. Rosie, at least, could be trusted to keep a watch on the interests of Paul Berners-Levine, as well as on my own family secret.

Part Two

THE SEARCH

And any action
Is a step to the block, to the fire, down
  the sea's throat
Or to an illegible stone: and that is
  where we start

T. S. ELIOT

1

I HAD been crazy to walk out on Harold Goldworthy—to lose the friendly security of Cliff's End because of a stupid flare-up with a middle-aged woman over a girl of eighteen and a boy of eleven.

Here I was, a "silly miserable bastard" as Keith Figgis would say, sitting alone in an empty house. Alone with my thoughts. Alone except for my mother's fussy furniture hemming me in. Alone, without family commitments or family connections of any kind. A man without purpose.

Sombrely, I worked through the debit side of my decision. No work. No qualification for work except a modest Oxford degree in History. More significant, no desire to stay in teaching or to apply for a Teacher Training course which might guarantee some sort of future in the profession. Worst of all, no ideas for the future beyond quitting the house in Maidstone which I'd already instructed our solicitors to sell.

In a wretched state of mind, I posted Christmas cards to Diana Murray, Rosie Ashcroft, the Goldworthys and—as a late thought came to me—to the Berners-Levine family. Then I made a final tour of the house, wondering whether I was right to get rid of its contents, but certain, too, that I had to escape from all the past associations it contained.

I looked idly through the drawers in mother's desk. Everything was in perfect order—bank statements; telephone, gas and electricity accounts; a list of shares and National Savings held by the bank; the papers concerned with the winding-up of the family business, all neatly filed and ticketed.

My only surprise came when, in a separate drawer, I uncovered the notes Mother had made prior to our holiday in the Welsh Marches. I had seen them before in their original form: but there was now plenty of evidence to show that they had been recently reread and edited: handwritten emendations, additional notes dating from her visit to Ockenham, and finally a couple of foolscap pages, speculating on my interest in the village and its inhabitants.

"I don't understand," she had written in her bold handwriting, "why Richard takes the place so seriously. Sometimes—I noted it especially after the Oxford visit—he seems obsessed with the personality of this priest he conjured up on holiday. Is there some hereditary connection? I've checked Richard's original birth certificate which is registered at Ashford where the mother, Margaret Jones, was resident before she settled in Australia. There's no suggestion of any link with Ockenham. Yet, something in Ockenham church seemed to force me to tell Richard about his birth. I just don't understand . . ."

A moment later, I came upon the birth certificate confirming the name of my natural mother as Margaret Jones. There was, of course, no reference to the father's name, and one could only conclude that the young woman had left the country soon after I had been legally adopted some twenty-five years before.

There and then I decided never to attempt to trace my real mother. I kept the certificate along with the other papers that had accumulated in the Maidstone house. But something or someone—call it self-imposed loneliness, if you like—prompted me to ring the Wotton Arms and book a room for the Christmas holiday. At that moment, Ockenham seemed the only home I had; or, at least, the only place where I could be alone without feeling lonely.

And that's how it worked out from the moment the Italian woman, Luisa Baker, ushered me into an ample room on the first floor of the Wotton Arms. Double bed, armchair, writing table, lots of space . . . exactly what I wanted. Main meals downstairs, she said: but would I be happy with a continental breakfast served in my room? It was with a feeling of relief and gratitude that I unpacked my case, switched on the table lamp and settled with a book into the easy chair.

Yet my solitude was soon to be disturbed. On that same evening, I was called to the phone.

"Monty Berners-Levine speaking. Richard Eveleigh? My God, you've taken a bit of finding. Tried Goldworthy's school, then your Maidstone house . . . tried the police . . . all useless . . . then this hunch from young Paul . . . No need to explain. Wanted a bit of solitude, eh? But you also want to be free of teaching? Yes, I understand. Now look. I think I've got a job for you. Change of scene. New life. Get away from the old school routine. Right? Me taking a chance? Not at all, my dear boy. It's you who will be chancing your arm. Anyway, will see you at Number 84 after lunch on 27th December. Got the address? Fine. More details when we meet. The boys and my wife send their greetings. Goodbye."

The phone went dead. In two minutes flat, with old Berners-Levine making the running and me jerking out monosyllabic replies, I had apparently applied for a job with a property tycoon. Or had I? Let me get to the other side of Christmas, I thought. Time enough to decide whether to work for the Berners-Levine outfit. Time enough, too, to work out how young Paul located me. Dates back, I suppose, to our Sunday visit to Ockenham. Pure chance? Or are these eleven-year-olds more sensitive to mood and atmosphere than teachers or parents ever realise?

Christmas at a village pub is a very different experience from Christmas at a London or seaside hotel—less festive and contrived, more homely and natural. The Wotton Arms was only different to the extent that, in these post-war years, Luisa had established a local reputation for first-class Italian cooking—meals being served in a restaurant with space for sixteen diners, which was entered from the bar where I had first met Ted Baker. There were no special facilities for guests apart from the three bedrooms and mod. con. on the first floor, so that the only common meeting-place was the bar. It appeared that I was the only resident guest except for a severely dressed old lady who was soon to be introduced to me as *La Nonna*—the grandmother.

In this part of Kent there is an unwritten law that on Christmas Day a publican serves no food and closes at 2 p.m., so that he can enjoy the rest of the day with his family and friends. The point had been hesitantly made to me on the phone when

I booked the room, but within twenty-four hours of my arrival Luisa told me that the Baker family would be delighted for me to join them for the evening meal on Christmas Day if I had no other plans. I accepted the invitation gratefully and spent the morning of Christmas Eve in Canterbury, making some hasty purchases—a scarf for Luisa, a tie for Ted, a spanner for the elder boy who wanted to know all about the inside of my car, a book for the girl and a Dinky car for the little boy. That—and a selection of sweets and cigarettes for stray participants in Luisa's Christmas feast—completed my Christmas purchases.

Christmas Day dawned fine and comparatively warm. I made a routine visit to the early Communion service at the village church, noting that the Major and various members of his family were present. I slipped away afterwards but surprised myself by returning at eleven o'clock for a family service which had attracted a crowd of children armed with Christmas presents as well as those adults who were not preparing the Christmas feasting. Various strangers greeted me. Back again at the pub, I found that Luisa had, unasked, placed in my bedroom a plate of beef sandwiches, a basket of fruit and a half bottle of Verdicchio, accompanied by a Christmas card signed by all the family. What a charming Italian gesture to find in a Kent village!

After lunch, a ten-mile walk seemed an essential preparation for Luisa's evening party: and so I started up the village street, and followed the path my mother and I had once taken through the great park. When I reached the oast house and the Dower House cottages, I continued upstream by the river bank, until I reached the western boundary of the Mortimer-Wotton land, returning by a circuitous route that took me through the hamlet of Little Ockenham. Eventually, I found my way back to the Wotton Arms by a lane that re-entered the village at its eastern limit.

It's a strange thing to say, but though I met no people on that walk, I never felt alone. As I crossed the fields and passed the scattered dwellings in the valley, I was conscious, everywhere, of the continuing life in this little community: the smoke spiralling from cottage chimneys, the evidence of children and Christmas decorations in the windows: and beyond the houses, the orderliness of the winter planting and the music of the stream lapping over stones and swishing round the willows' roots. Even the oaks and beeches, standing sentinel in the park, seemed to have their appointed places. Timelessness was here, so that "world without end", that prayerful incantation I'd heard in the church, was suddenly filled with real meaning.

Subconsciously, my senses were aware of a new picture projected onto the screen of my mind—a composite picture of this fourteenth-century village and the great family the priest had served.

This priest, Nicholas Maidstone. A perfect example of the Faithful Steward. Serving the fourteenth-century Mortimers at Court and Dover and Wigmore. Loyal, like his masters, to the Black Prince and his son, Richard II. Involved with Wycliff: joining him, perhaps, on missions to Europe . . . how this valley of Ockenham sparked the imagination.

On firm ground again with Nicholas returning (why, why, why?) to the safety of insignificant, hidden Ockenham, but emerging again to march with Wat Tyler and the villagers to London . . .

In my ears the countryside echoed with the ominous rhythm of marching feet, the Kentish rebels moving inexorably forward to Maidstone and the final, swift assault on the capital . . . disciplined men, with purpose in their feet,

Left, left . . . left, right, left.
Go, Richard, go . . . to London, go:
Away from teaching rich men's sons.
Away, away from Ockenham's peace.
To London go where poor men strive.
Set your course. To London, go.

Was this drumming in my ears a command from outside? Or was I, Richard Eveleigh, on the point of deliberate decision at last?

With an effort, I shook the insistent rhythm from my head. But, for a few moments of time, I knew I had been close in spirit to those Kentish rebels of other days. What was it Rosie Ashcroft had said? If life stretches into the future, doesn't it also imply a link with the years before you were born?

As I re-entered the village, the fourteenth-century picture faded into the gathering darkness of the winter sky.

Who, indeed, could be more in the present than I was that night at Luisa's Christmas party? Ted Baker, slow-smiling and authoritative, took the head of the table and carved the turkey: but, truth to tell, Italy had taken over the English Christmas at the Wotton Arms. I was placed next to Luisa when she had time to sit down. The grandmother, *La Nonna*, sat on Ted's right, in the place of honour, with the three Baker children on one side of the long table, the other side occupied by myself and two Italians, Antonio and Franca Battista, who were employed at the Great House as gardener and cook. We drank a toast to the grandmother: then to Luisa, provider of the feast. A constant babble of Italian kept the grandmother in excellent humour, but the party often reverted to English for my benefit. Indeed, it was from Antonio's broken English that I learnt more about the Master of the Great House.

121

"Ah, ah, *il Comandante*," he said, emitting an audible burp, "Zee Major, *capito*? 'E save old Ted's life in Italy, *non e vero*, Ted? And then Ted and 'is army enter Firenze and 'e captures *la bella Luisa* eh? But after Sangro battle *il Comandante* is sick man, ordered to stay in Ravello where 'e buys villa and finds me and Franca. Ah, ah, *c'e molto gentile, il Comandante*." And Antonio belched again. "Franca, she arrange with zee Major for old Gwynedd Morgan to stay tonight at big house and guard our *bambino*. You no meet Gwynedd, Mister Ricardo? She is Mister Garage Morgan's sister. Long ago she nurse zee Major when 'e was baby. Now she nurse our little son. *Salute al Comandante*." Rising a little unsteadily Antonio insisted on clinking glasses with everybody in the Major's honour before draining his glass.

About eleven o'clock, the old lady rose from the table. Her gesture was as positive as a referee's final whistle. I said goodnight to each member of the party with a special bow of deference to the grandmother. Her presence had fascinated me throughout the evening: though she had spoken little, I

122

was sure her ears were alert and her eyes all-seeing. She had watched me as carefully as she had watched the grandchildren who waited on her during the meal. I left the party, deeply impressed by the serenity and authority of this old lady. I would have loved a grandmother of my own.

Next morning I settled my account with Ted and Luisa: and Michael Baker, the elder boy to whom I'd given the adjustable spanner, joined me in the car park where my ancient Morris was showing an early morning reluctance to spark. Eventually, it came to noisy life with Michael holding the choke and me sweating away at the starting handle. Satisfied at last that the car was sparking on all four cylinders, Michael stuffed my suitcase and books into the back and closed the driver's door on me. As he said goodbye, he suddenly checked his speech.

"Oh, I nearly forgot," he said, pulling a piece of paper from his pocket. "The grandmother commanded me to give you a special message. *La Nonna*, she writes: '*Buon Anno, Signor Eveleigh. Ella spera di reincontrarla di nuovo dopo che hai iniziato il suo nuovo lavoro a Londra*'."

123

Michael, his eyes twinkling, read the Italian off a scrubby piece of paper with positively Florentine fluency: and then added for my benefit, with a bow and a flourish, "Which means, Signor Ricardo, that my Italian granny wishes you the best of luck in the New Year and hopes to meet you again when you've settled into your new job in London."

The boy laughed as he waved farewell. And I left for London convinced that the old lady was reinforcing the message I'd heard in the fields on Christmas Day.

2

NUMBER 84. You could not miss the figures—boldly black on white entrance pillars, placed at each end of a wall which marked the frontage of an imposing Victorian mansion.

Situated in a quiet road off Clapham Common, the house was a classic example of "late Victorian". It was all there: the steps leading up to the wide front door, the semi-basement kitchen quarters, the maids' bedrooms on the third floor: and between the upper and lower extremes of the servants' back staircase, a set of fine high-ceilinged rooms in which a wealthy Victorian family would have been proud to reside around the turn of the century. It was easy to picture the prosperity of the first owner—the more so, because Number 84 was in excellent repair and stood out in sharp contrast from its half-derelict neighbours which had so far escaped the destruction of enemy bombing or post-war development.

I backed my car into some garage accommodation to the left of the house, behind which I glimpsed a spacious well-timbered garden, and mounted the steps to the black-painted front door with its polished brass knocker and letter box. A middle-aged woman with grey hair and a rather sad face answered my knock.

"You'll be Mr. Eveleigh," she said, as she ushered me into a small book-lined room to the left of the hall. "Mr. Berners-Levine is expecting you."

A few minutes later Monty Berners-Levine conducted me across the hall into a large reception room which had been converted into the office headquarters of Berninko Properties. It contained two desks, a number of filing cabinets and an assortment of chairs. Everything was clean and orderly, matching the upkeep of the house and the proprietor's blue pin-stripe suit, white shirt and discreet tie.

He offered me a seat on one side of the bigger of the two desks and then took his place on the far side. He launched briskly into a description of the job—part book-keeper and part house-tutor to the boys, he said. He asked no leading questions, taking it for granted that I would accept the appointment. His only inquiry concerned my salary at Cliff's End. When I told him, he emitted a curious whistle between his teeth and promptly offered me twice the salary Harold Goldworthy had been paying.

He also informed me that a rent-free bedroom was available to me and I would be welcome to eat with the family. "Only one word of warning," he added. "Mrs. Binder—that's the German lady who opened the door to you—is a superb cook, but very set in her ways and easily put out. She'll expect to know your plans before nine-thirty each morning. Her husband, Fred, is a first-class mechanic and gardener, and with Trudi's aid virtually runs the establishment. That's about the size of it except for a 'daily' who comes under Trudi's command."

When I told Monty I had no knowledge of book-keeping, he waved aside my objection. "Not to worry. A short City and Guilds Course will put you right. Your predecessor knew everything about figures, but the boys thought he was intolerably dull: and Fred and Trudi didn't like him either. So he had to go. Didn't fit, if you see what I mean."

I asked him about the boys. "Ah, that's the nub of the matter," he replied. "That's why we need you. Fact is, Hermina and I have to travel a fair amount overseas while the boys are at school. And it don't seem right to expect the Binders to be responsible for their good behaviour while we're away. So we thought of you. Hermina's idea, really. Or was it young Paul's? Can't remember exactly." And Monty Berners gave me a friendly smile as he led me to a well-appointed bedroom on the second floor.

I spent the first three months of my time at Number 84 in learning about Berninko Properties and studying for my City and Guilds Certificate in book-keeping and office management. But Monty was right. The management and supervision of Berninko Properties was simplicity itself.

By comparison with the other property empires of those days, Berninko was a modest affair: three blocks of flats in three prosperous suburbs of South London and a number of shop properties in the same localities. There were no capital developments on hand: and rents reached Number 84 with commendable regularity from three separate agents. I had little more to do than keep the records and bank the cheques. By the end of that year, I had time on my hands.

In addition to my salary, the Company paid the office cleaner's wages and the salaries and pensions of Fred and Trudi Binder. It met a very fair share of the rates and upkeep of the house, which was owned by Hermina. And it possessed three cars, perfectly maintained by Fred: a Rolls for Monty, a Peugeot for his wife and a Morris 1100 for general use. Monty and Hermina seemed content with modest salaries but received enormous expenses and travel allowances, chiefly concerned with their overseas activities—"This export game is very expensive, Richard, my boy: and you have to play it properly if you play it at all."

Whether the Berners-Levines played properly or improperly, I was too immature to ask—I was, after all, no more than a book-keeper. But I knew that by the time Berninko had met the interest on the considerable bank loan secured by its properties in England, the profits were too modest to bring much joy to the Inland Revenue.

Almost in spite of myself, I liked what I saw of Monty and Hermina, acknowledging that they were part of a world of which I had no previous knowledge. They were, of course, vulgarly ostentatious—especially the outsize Hermina with her bizarre taste in chunky jewellery. Though they were Jews by birth, they professed no religious affiliation to their ancestral faith. They spent much of the year in five-star hotels in the West Indies and Spain where they also had property interests. But when they were in England, they were regular patrons of Covent Garden and the newly opened Festival Hall as well as the best West End restaurants.

It would be easy to dismiss them as totally amoral. Yet, while they were over-indulgent to themselves and their children, they were more than generous to their staff. Take Fred and Trudi Binder, for example. Monty had found them after the war, living in exile and great poverty in the East End, and shrewdly decided that they must be blessed with intelligence as well as courage ever to have reached London. He had hired them on the spot, paid them well, and been rewarded by their total loyalty and affection.

When I arrived at Number 84, Fred and Trudi had assumed complete charge of the house administration, and for the moment I was happy to be one of the Company. In a sense I shared with the Binders a common sense of gratitude since I, too, had been rescued from a dead-end job by Monty Berners-Levine.

By the autumn of 1957 Paul had joined Daniel at Westminster School and the conversation at Number 84 constantly reverted to the people we'd known at Cliff's End—the Goldworthys, Keith Figgis, Aunt Edna, Diana Murray and, most often, Rosie Ashcroft who was Paul's special love. The latter's enjoyment of music and growing skill as a pianist already pointed to his future career. But Daniel, a precociously clever boy approaching his sixteenth birthday, was likely to provide his parents with a few problems.

One evening he reported that he and

some of his classmates had been sent on what he called "a sociological project". "Slumming," he added by way of explanation. "Wapping, Isle of Dogs, Limehouse, the Highway, Cable Street—you name it: and for good measure, a ration of racial unrest. Chinese, Bengalis, Sikhs, West Indians and Jews from half the world: an all-nations set-up living cheek by jowl with the beer-drinkers and betting shop patrons of Cockney London. I reckoned that with my face I might easily be numbered among the unwanted settlers, if I stayed down there."

It was a fairly typical school-boy remark. But the cynical throw-away line could not disguise the fact that this particular visit to the East End had given birth to another angry young man. Somewhere, Daniel had been reminded of his Jewish origins.

He changed the subject, as if to hide the crack exposed in his private defences. "But here's something to interest you, Richard. Returning by way of Whitechapel Underground, I ran straight into the lovely Diana Murray, doing her shopping at the barrows opposite the station. Told me she's working for a bloke in Wapping. What do you know about that, eh?"

It's hard to explain my excitement at the news Daniel retailed so casually. Diana and I had not been in touch since our exchange of Christmas cards. I only knew that she had embarked on a secretarial course at Guildford. Luckily Daniel had been given her address: and the second the boys left Number 84 the following morning, I found her phone number.

I tried to sound calm but my hand was shaking as I waited for her to reach the phone and she must have heard the excitement in my voice. Yet the moment she answered, I knew Diana had not changed: that we would meet again in London just as we had once met at Cliff's End. There would be the same easy companionship, the same common interests, a sort of natural alliance.

That same evening I "signed off" with Trudi and made the first of many journeys from SW4. to E1.—at first a tedious journey by Underground from Clapham Common to Whitechapel via Charing Cross, and later in a Berninko car which Fred Binder procured for my use after selling my old Morris for scrap. Fred was something of a perfectionist. He didn't like a lame horse in the stables at Number 84.

I wasn't exactly surprised that Diana had gravitated to London. Most secretaries in the Home Counties tend to do so, and Diana had the additional incentive that she was unhappy at home. But there were to be no plush city offices for Diana. I found she had deliberately attached herself to a parson called John Spencer who ran some sort of a Mission in Wapping.

The job gave her free digs and pin-money wages in return for endless hours of typing, filing, washing up and cleaning up: even on occasion helping out Mrs. Spencer with a group of three- and four-year-olds who played at the Club while their mothers were at work.

I began to help Diana with her interminable chores whenever I was free: and in the next eighteen months, during our over-the-sink conversations, I learnt more about her family. She was by many years the youngest member of it, with two older brothers married and working overseas. But while she was fond of her elderly father, a doctor with a Surrey practice, she was in constant disagreement with a dominating and opinionated mother. Mother, she assured me, was the spur that drove her to Broadstairs and now to London.

"But why Dockland?" I asked, and suddenly she let herself go.

"Can't you understand?" she said. "I can't stick my mother's world a moment longer—the money talk, the interminable bridge parties, the heated swimming pools and the rest of the status symbols. I want to know how the real world lives: and by heavens I'm learning more at this place than I ever learnt at school—or Broadstairs! Don't you sometimes feel the same way?"

Her eyes lit up with a suffragette's zeal. There was a sort of "dare you" look which enhanced her natural beauty. Society conventions were irrelevant. I was seeing the real Diana and she was seeing something that young Daniel had also glimpsed on his "sociological project".

This outburst was more than usually explicit, but she knew from earlier talks at Broadstairs that she was baiting me in an area where I had no defences. I think she knew that, unless I'd been brain-washed by Monty Berners-Levine, I should, sooner or later, rebel against my present occupation. She knew . . . she knew . . . , but she was much too clever to press the point. Some girls of twenty-two are very mature.

With Monty and Hermina prospecting in Barbados, and the two boys at school, my days at Number 84 would have become tedious but for the presence of Fred and Trudi Binder. Fred, a Pole in everything but name, had qualified as a lawyer in pre-war Poland and, with the aid of a Roman Catholic priest, smuggled himself onto a Gdynia-London boat at the time of the German invasion in 1939. He had met Trudi in Whitechapel where she was working for a West End tailor—a sweat-shop, I was led to understand, similar to the home from which young Monty Levine (no Berners then!) had escaped a few years earlier.

The Binders evinced no desire to return to Poland or East Germany. They felt safe, they said, at Number 84, and avoided all contact with other fellow nationals in London. On the other hand they retained many close friendships in the East End. They often spoke of the wonderful people with whom they had endured the London blitz. Brave as the Poles themselves, Fred used to tell me. Brave as the Polish airmen and the Podolski Lancers who raised the Polish flag above the Monastery at Cassino. London's East End could receive no higher praise.

But Fred had a mind for the present, too. Things in Stepney and Whitechapel had changed, he told me, since he and Trudi lived there. Ugly things we didn't see in the war—crime syndicates, bully-boys ganging up against Asians, West Indians, Jews . . . You watch it, Richard, you and your girl, and don't take sides if you want to live happily ever after.

Fred, rather pleased with his mastery of English phrases, put his head back into the bonnet of the car he was tuning. It was only later that I remembered his warning.

For the moment, I found myself contrasting the Binders' struggle to survive with my free-wheeling existence. What could I show for my life? A little education, a few passing acquaintances: perhaps, giving myself the benefit of the doubt, a certain ability to get small boys interested in their work. What a miserable contrast with Trudi and Fred . . . And what a contrast, too, with those fourteenth-century characters who had paraded before me at Ockenham and who, in times of idleness, continued to invade my mind.

Sometimes, when I was alone at No. 84, the poor priest, Nicholas, almost became my conscience—or should I say companion. During these under-occupied days I began to gain a clear picture of the little priest, almost as if I were developing a photograph from a dark negative. He would stand beside me, a boy from nowhere. A clever boy, devoted to Roger Mortimer, to whom he had vowed his service and something more than loyalty. It was a clear case of hero worship: and his hero had appointed him to teach his son, Edmund, so that when the young man became a great officer of the Crown, the priest-tutor shared the privileges of the king's counsellors.

In my imagination I began to grow familiar with the characters surrounding Nicholas. The single portrait became a group, the snapshot changed to panorama. With fascinating clarity I could pick out and delineate these heroes of fourteenth-century England. They stepped out of the history books and I found myself measuring their achievements, their daring, their loves and hates: above all, their youth. There they stood, commanding the king's armies, dictating the nation's policy, conducting international negotiations at my age, Diana's age, Daniel's age . . .

Was Nicholas telling me that the young men and women of today were waiting too long to grasp power and make their influence felt? Or was the final picture, emerging from this hazy negative of chivalry and church building and peasants in revolt, something more personal, something directed at me? Was there reproach, as well as grief, in the eyes of the young priest? Was I no different from Gaunt and his lackeys, helping the selfish and the self-indulgent to acquire money and abuse power?

That same evening, Daniel, who was going through the inevitable Marxist phase of every clever sixteen-year-old, added to the feeling of guilt sown in my mind by the

Ockenham priest. "Richard," he said at dinner, "how much longer are you going to stick this racket at Number 84?"

"What do you mean?" I said. "You're a bit hot under the collar, aren't you? One of your left-wing friends been nudging you?"

"Oh, come off it, man. Give me credit for being able to think for myself. Don't tell me you can't see that father is a prince of fiddlers, with mother a dedicated second fiddle to keep him company. For God's sake, wake up and wipe your eyes. It's three years since you were an innocent schoolmaster. Surely you can *think*, as well as keep the books of this bogus concern."

It's no good arguing with a scholarship type like Daniel. Far better to change the subject. So I asked him how he saw his own future.

"Oxford first," he said decisively, "and then journalism or politics. Someone has to put the world to rights and rid England of its social parasites." Already I could see Daniel with a Cabinet post in a left-wing administration or even as chief assistant to Orwell's Big Brother.

But when I retired to bed that night, I stayed awake for a long time, worrying, not about Daniel or his family, but about my dithering, indecisive self.

3

DANIEL'S argument was too close to the truth for comfort. It was time I needed—time to sort myself out. With him and his brother due to join their parents for a summer holiday on the Costa Brava, I figured I could easily escape from Clapham Common. Fred and Trudi were entirely competent to look after Number 84 and deal with incoming cheques and correspondence.

So I rang Ted Baker at the Wotton Arms, only to be told that the place was in the hands of the decorators: there was no room at the inn. But Ted must have sensed my disappointment for, after a slight hesitation, he said he would make some inquiries about alternative accommodation in Ockenham.

Sure enough, he rang back the same evening to say he'd had a word with Evan Morgan, his friend at the garage opposite the pub. Evan had consulted his sister, Gwynedd, up at the Dower House cottages.

And Gwynedd, fully armed with my credentials, had persuaded a Miss Millicent Taylor to provide me with a fortnight's lodging at her house in Little Ockenham. Ted was anxious to reassure me.

"You're in luck," he said. "Beautiful little thatched cottage. Spotlessly clean. Nice and quiet. Good English cooking."

"And Miss Taylor?"

"Good Heavens, I'd forgotten. You've never met her, have you? She's a character, I can tell you. Apart from the Major, she's our best-known citizen. Long ago, she was headmistress of the village school—a great friend of the Major's old grandmother, Mrs. Mortimer-Wotton. She's getting on now, rising seventy I'd say: but very sprightly. Knows everybody's history, and hasn't an enemy in the world. We all call her 'Miss Millie' like the kids used to do at school."

Millicent Taylor's house in Little Ockenham proved to be one of a row of small cottages, set back from the lane by a strip of mown grass, and distinguished from its neighbours as much by the neatness of its garden as by its thatched roof.

The old lady who greeted me was small

of stature and grey-haired, but brisk in her walk and precise in her speech. The interior of the cottage, neat and orderly, seemed an exact reflection of its owner's character.

Her face was unlined by care and her eyes were alive with the understanding of old age. And, as I came to know her, I discovered she also possessed the born teacher's skill for coaxing the background thinking out of her pupil—or, in my case, her lodger.

Certainly, she knew instinctively that I was something of a loner. Almost casually, she told me that she had, as a girl, looked after an invalid mother and so, in a sense, had loneliness thrust upon her. But that was all past history, she assured me. "If you're a schoolmistress in a village like Ockenham and live there as long as I have done, you know and are known by all the people you want to know—from the Mortimer-Wottons to the Bakers inclusive."

And of course she quickly discovered my interest in Ockenham Church.

"There's more to its history," she told me, "than you find in the guide book. That is limited to verifiable facts and dates—dry as dust. It leaves out the exciting bits connected with the family up at the Great House."

"How do you mean?"

"Well, take the two brasses in the chancel which you see from the communion rail. The guide book correctly identifies them as fourteenth-century memorials to Lady Edwina Mortimer and her son, Thomas: but it doesn't record the rest of the story. The Lady Edwina was Chatelaine of the Great House at the time of the Peasants' Revolt, her husband having been killed at Poitiers when serving with the Black Prince: and she was clearly a woman of great ability and exceptional courage. Her son, Thomas, was knighted by the boy king, Richard II, for supporting him and London's Mayor Walworth in the confrontation with the rebels at Smithfield. Unhappily, Thomas's friendship with Richard angered the king's powerful uncle, John of Gaunt—the more so because the House of Mortimer stood in the way of the Lancastrian succession to the crown. And Thomas, although stemming from a junior branch of the family, had been educated with the great Marcher Lord, young Edmund Mortimer, who was the Black Prince's protégé and by this time Earl Marshal of England. So when Gaunt, in spite of the king's promises of pardon to the Kentish rebels, sent Commissioners into the County to arrest the ring-leaders, he also ordered them to visit the Great House on a trumped-up charge that Lady Edwina had falsified the Poll tax accounts for the Hundred of Ockenham. Thomas and three companions challenged Gaunt's thugs but were eventually overwhelmed. They were killed in front of the house where the rose garden is now laid out—but their resistance gave Lady Edwina and her daughters time to reach the church where the terrified villagers had also sought refuge."

Miss Millie paused in her narration, looking up to see if she was holding my attention. Then she continued. "But the story doesn't end there. Legend has it that the people in the church were saved by the bravery of a young priest, devoted to Lady Edwina, who deliberately left the church and walked unarmed towards the marauders, believing they would respect his cloth. The poor man was hacked to death in the churchyard and, because it was sacred ground, his mutilated body was hurled over the surrounding wall into the field outside. The last sound the villagers heard that day was the clatter of Gaunt's men riding away, down the village street to their next assignment. In those days even violent men were afraid of committing sacrilege."

Suddenly, I blurted out, "So that was how Nicholas Maidstone died?"

"Yes, indeed." The old lady spoke very calmly, as if unaware of the excitement in my voice. "That was the priest's name." And she moved across the room to fetch some embroidery on which she was working. As she returned to her chair, she added, "One day, perhaps, you'll have a chance to browse in the Major's library. It holds some strange relics and documents. I often used to look at them in the pre-war days when his dear grandmother was alive. But they are an unusual family, the Mortimer-Wottons. They seem to take the past for granted and are only interested in the present and future. I suppose that's what makes them different from the other great families round here."

The next day, sensing my interest in the village, Miss Millie suggested I should join the specially enlisted hands who were helping with the gathering and grading of the early potatoes for the London market. I would learn more about the locals in the fields than I would in her cottage or "the Wotton".

"And you'll get some money as well as exercise," she added in her practical way. "And better company than on your solo walks and excursions to Canterbury."

It seemed a good idea. A word from Miss Millie, and I was signed up by Amos Williams at the Home Farm which lies behind the Great House. For the rest of my holiday I was collected daily by a Land-Rover which conveyed me and a variety of young women and teenagers to the potato fields on the high ground at the western limits of the Mortimer-Wotton land. Each evening I would return to the thatched cottage in Little Ockenham, with an aching back and full of stories about my fellow-workers.

Most of them were wives or children of the regular farm hands, and Miss Millie would give names and homes to the people I described. "That's Susan Peck," she would say. "Pretty girl, but comes from a difficult family. Always in trouble with money." Or she would laugh indulgently about Amos and Margie Williams's children. "Naughty like their mother, but bright little buttons—all five of them. I doubt if any of them will stay in farming, whatever Amos thinks."

My fortnight's break from office routine at Number 84 passed all too quickly. But it was time enough for Miss Millie, who had solved her own problem of loneliness, to show me how to solve mine. As I said goodbye to the neat little woman, I felt a great affection for her. I was fascinated by her friendly and calm authority. I had seen the same qualities in *La Nonna* at Luisa's Christmas party. But for Miss Millie my feelings went deeper—love, I think, as well as respect. If you have no mother, a grandmother can be a very useful substitute.

But it was really John Spencer in Wapping who finally made me change direction.

Diana's boss came from a legal family, his father heading a well-established firm of family solicitors in Lincoln's Inn. John had qualified as a solicitor and in 1939 was about to join his father when war was declared. Being a Territorial, he was catapulted into uniform and ended the war as a staff officer in North-West Europe. After VE day something or somebody caused him to give up the law in favour of the Church.

I picked up John's background from Diana who had it from his wife, Susie. What the world and I encountered was a somewhat unconventional parson, only seen in a dog-collar when he was taking a service. An athletic type, he kept fit by walking. In an area bounded to the north by the Commercial Road, and to the south by the Thames, stretching from St. Katharine's Dock to the entrance to the Grand Union Canal, there was scarcely a street or alley he did not know. In Cable Street and the Highway he was a familiar figure with his dark hair, sallow face and slow smile. At the Mission his work-rate was tremendous but, possibly because of his legal training, he never appeared to hurry though his speed of thought was as marked as the pace of his footsteps. He was a hard man to keep up with: but we all liked him, and his wife and school-age children adored him.

One evening when I turned up at the Club, he called out "Hi, Richard. You here again? Ever thought of a change of job?" No mention of Diana, though I'm sure he knew that for me Diana was a bigger attraction than the whole of Dockland put together. I laughed, but he went on, "I can always fix you up with something—teaching or book-keeping on our Appeals side. Or you can combine the two. We need full-time help in addition to our volunteers. Ask Diana. Or give it a thought in your big house in SW4. London has a different face in E1. and a different scale of rewards: but it's a darn sight more interesting than the property market, as seen from Clapham Common."

He didn't pursue the conversation, hurrying off to quell an incipient riot in a big room given over to some youngsters in the noisy age group. Nor did I reply. But I saw Diana watching me. "Well?" she said.

"Oh, I don't know," I replied. "I keep hearing the same story—from you, John

Spencer and Daniel Berners-Levine. You're all getting at me. Even Nicholas is in league with you, I believe." Diana looked so surprised, standing there in her trousers and open-necked shirt.

"Nicholas? Who is Nicholas? You've never told me about him."

"You'll only laugh at me, if I do," I said. "Anyway, Nicholas wouldn't understand this set-up. There were manor houses and farms in Stepney when he was alive." Diana was really intrigued and she looked more beautiful than any girl I'd ever seen.

"Tell me, Richard, tell me about him," she pleaded.

"Only if you come with me to the place where he lived."

"Done," she said.

I don't know what happened next. Perhaps she saw a new light in my eye or heard a new note in my voice—she was very sensitive to sight and sound. Suddenly she came into my arms, the softness of her breasts pressed against me. Our lips parted as we kissed . . . my hands were touching her hair, her body . . . She was no longer the schoolgirl of Broadstairs or the secretary who had abandoned a comfortable home in favour of Dockland. In my arms was a new creature, somebody who passionately wanted me, as I wanted her.

We parted for a moment and looked into each other's eyes—hers alight and shining through tears. "Well?" she said with that funny little shy smile I loved.

"We get married," I replied. "We go in search of Nicholas. And when we find him we bring him back to a Stepney flat and show him how our world lives."

One says silly things on occasions like this, I'm told. They sound silly to everybody but the girl you love. There in the canteen kitchen at John Spencer's club, we were aware of nobody but ourselves—and maybe, Nicholas, who had brought us together.

4

IN the days that followed our engagement, Diana and I were, I suppose,
as self-centred and inconsiderate as any
story-book lovers. We were in love and we
lived for each other alone. Our thoughts,
hopes, fears, bodies—we wanted to share
everything together.

For me, Diana possessed a quality—
perhaps it was her virginal innocence—
which excited in me a sort of fear as well
as desire. It was a feeling I cannot pretend to define. Back at Cliff's End—how
long ago it seemed—Mary Winter had
permitted me to be her lover: and I had
possessed her body, knowing I was not her
first lover—perhaps no more than the latest
plaything for an afternoon in the sun. We
had parted with hardly a backward glance.
I had no idea what had happened to her
since she had left the school.

But with Diana it was different. To keep
her for ever was to possess something so
precious as to be almost sacred. Back in the

bedroom at Number 84, I would ask myself again and again why this young and lovely girl, with a mind of her own, should want to give herself to a misfit like Richard Eveleigh. Yet I knew she did. I knew she was alive with the same longing that filled my heart.

John and Susie Spencer must, I think, have guessed that a long engagement would be intolerable. Certainly it was the Spencers who, in their separate ways, persuaded us that it would be wrong for us to live together unmarried: and equally wrong to get married secretly without the prior consent of Diana's parents.

So, one Saturday, we arranged to visit Dr. and Mrs. Murray. I collected Diana from Wapping in the Berninko Morris. Talking and laughing, we crossed Vauxhall Bridge, threaded our way through the South London suburbs and headed for the Surrey hills. The July sun was shining from a clear blue sky as we left the main road short of Guildford and saw with delight the multiple greens of trees and fields which seemed a world away from Wapping and Stepney. But as we approached the

Murrays' house, our happiness changed to apprehension.

Diana was sure the day would go wrong and her anxiety infected me. She thought she would embarrass me: or, worse still, I would embarrass her. She put her hand lightly on my knee by way of reassurance.

"Darling, don't look so worried," she said. "I know you're supposed to ask father's permission: but I'll fix him. He really is a lovely man."

"And mother?"

"Oh, mother? Well, I guess she'll get you by herself whatever I say—you see if she doesn't. And then she'll start chattering about a thousand irrelevancies—poor darling, she can't help it—about white weddings, bridesmaids, choirs, and a tent for the reception. But don't you commit yourself, love. Mother's ideas for the Great Occasion are not mine. And why should father be saddled with a vast bill for something we don't want?"

Diana's warning was bang on target. After a rather stilted tea party, Dr. Murray went off to tour the garden with Diana: and I was left with Mrs. Murray. I could not think of anything to say. I was, indeed, speculating as to how this good-looking woman had reared a daughter with such an entirely different set of values, when the inquisition began.

"Now tell me, Richard, about yourself. You first met Diana, you say, at Cliff's End? Yes: and then there was some sort of disagreement which caused you to give up school-mastering? No, nothing to do with Diana . . . I quite understand . . . just that school life did not suit you. And this property company you are working for now— you see a future there? Berninko isn't a quoted company, is it?"

So the woman had been consulting the *Financial Times* for guidance. Sitting on one of those uncomfortable white garden chairs that are supposed to look like wrought-iron, my answers were monosyllabic. I must have given my future mother-in-law the impression that I was unlikely to hold down any job, lucrative or otherwise, for she suddenly switched from career to family.

"I was so sorry," she said, "to hear from Diana that you had lost both your parents. How very sad."

I could stand it no longer. Mrs. Murray

was getting me rattled just as Diana had predicted. Deliberate or accidental, this delicate probing must be brought to an end. I felt an awful compulsion to take it "head on".

"Not actually my parents, Mrs. Murray. Diana was speaking of the childless couple who adopted me as a baby. I'm afraid I've no idea who or where my real parents are. My adopted family were very kind to me and gave me a name and an education for which I shall always owe them thanks. But illegitimacy is something I've come to accept. It makes me all the more grateful to Diana for accepting me as she has."

I had intended to put an end to the conversation there and then. But as she rose from the table in obvious embarrassment, I felt thoroughly sorry for her and ashamed of my own pigheadedness. "Please," I stuttered ineptly, "I can't help my family background. I really love Diana. Please don't worry about us."

Thank God, Dr. Murray reappeared at this moment, crossing the lawn arm-in-arm with Diana. They were both laughing.

"Diana's told me all about you," he said. "Says you're changing jobs to join the

Spencers in Wapping and settling for a council flat in the East End. Fair enough, if that's what you both want—and the very best of luck. Oh, one other thing, Richard. There's no need to ask me for my daughter's hand. Diana has already twisted my arm and told me all I need to know about Richard Eveleigh. Let's drink to the future." And the doctor bustled into the house, emerging a few moments later with a bottle of champagne.

We could surely leave him to comfort his wife in her disappointment about her daughter's choice. As Diana and his patients could confirm, Dr. Murray was a very understanding man as well as a good doctor.

A few weeks later, John Spencer officiated at our wedding in Wapping Church. It was just as Diana wished, the congregation consisting of her father and mother, the Spencer family, some members of the Club staff and a few of her friends.

To my surprise, however, a small posse of friends arrived to give me support. Weeks earlier, I had officially resigned from Berninko and returned the company car to

Fred Binder's keeping. But the Berners-Levine boys, who had been the first to learn about Diana, had been quick to spread the news about our forthcoming marriage.

Fred and Trudi Binder were the first to appear at the church, looking very smart indeed. A few minutes later, to my surprise and delight, Rosie Ashcroft and her two sons arrived, Paul having told them the time and place of the wedding. And such is the strength of the East Kent grapevine that telegrams reached us from the Goldworthys, Piers Bovill and Hugh and Margaret Dickinson. Best of all, I received a letter from Miss Millie two days before the wedding. It was written in the most beautiful handwriting I've ever seen, expressing the hope that I would in due course introduce my bride to her.

As for Daniel and Paul Berners-Levine, they raced up to the church with a squealing of brakes and a horn fanfare, as if to let the world know that Daniel had passed his driving test. They arrived a split second ahead of Diana and her father. After the service, at the party arranged for us by Susie Spencer, Daniel managed to draw me aside, looking the complete conspirator.

"The keys, guv," he said with a mock cockney accent, and handed me the familiar keyring of the Morris 1100. "Message from the Padrone in Zurich . . . says you are to tear up your railway tickets. Your car awaits you, good as new, tuned up for the honeymoon by Fred and wax-polished by Trudi."

I must have acted a bit dumb, for he added in his normal voice, "Don't look so surprised, man. The car is all yours, no strings attached. Presented with Berninko's compliments. And here's something for the petrol."

Laughing as he spoke, he handed me the keys, together with an envelope containing a cheque for £500 signed by Monty Berners-Levine. Apparently, when Daniel had told his parents in Switzerland that Diana and I were going to settle in Stepney, he struck a chord of memory in the heart of the Whitechapel tailor's son.

The gift even surprised Daniel by its generosity.

"You never know with father," he said —and there was honest admiration in the son's voice. "He simply told me that if you and Diana were determined to live in E1., you'd need a record player for comfort and a car for escape."

An hour later, Diana and I were on our way to Ockenham, sitting side by side in the familiar car. It never ran more smoothly or looked smarter than it did on that day of our wedding. I think of it still when I hear the have-nots railing at the wealthy. God knows they have reason to do so: but not all successful people are without a heart. Monty and Hermina were the most spontaneously generous people I've ever met.

5

THE Wotton Arms at Ockenham had always been our honeymoon destination: had I not promised to show Diana the place where Nicholas had first crossed my path? And, to my relief, Ted and Luisa Baker proved to be discreet and charming hosts, receiving us gravely as Mr. and Mrs. Richard Eveleigh, without any hint in their behaviour that we might be in the "just married" category.

As we undressed together on that first night, I am sure I was more nervous than my young bride, so concerned was I that we should come together easily and gently, without haste or hurt to Diana. But our first act of love was simply achieved. Next morning we woke in each other's arms, absurdly pleased with each other and eager to meet new horizons in each other's company.

It was on the following Monday on a windless, sunlit day, that Diana and I realised how much our love meant to us.

We had left "the Wotton", armed with one of Luisa's special lunches—a home-made quiche, I remember, with fruit, a thermos of coffee and a half-bottle of wine from Luisa's native Italy. We settled to our picnic beside a ridge of trees on the high ground that marks the southern boundary of the Mortimer-Wotton land. Below us lay the park we had just crossed. Close to the Lodge at the end of the beech avenue we could see a man mowing the cricket field: and the lake in the centre of our vision was teeming with bird life. To our right we looked down on the Great House—a lion couchant, guarding its territory: and to the left the valley of Ockenham stretched westward to the horizon. In the distance, we could see and hear a farm tractor chugging its way along the edge of a field. Across the stream that flowed down the valley to join the lake, the squat Norman tower of St. Dunstan's stood silhouetted on its little hill overlooking the people of Ockenham, as it had done for the past eight hundred years. And in the village nothing stirred.

We were dozing side by side in the sunshine, for how long I do not know. But I was suddenly conscious of my companion stirring. She changed her position very quietly, as if careful not to disturb me. Then her fingers touched mine and I looked up to meet Diana's eyes. She was leaning over me, her shirt unbuttoned, her lips parted in invitation. "I'm ready for you," she whispered. "Please, I want you to make love to me here, Richard my darling . . . please . . . I want you now." She lay back, pulling me towards her, her hand rousing me, urgently guiding me. I entered her body. For a moment which seemed an eternity, we waited. Then again she whispered, "My love, my own darling love, I want you so much . . . come to me . . . now." And there, in the perfection of a sun-kissed afternoon and the peace of the Kent countryside, the extent of our physical love was fully realised.

In a curious way, I have never forgotten that it was on Diana's invitation that we made love together that day. From that moment I was no longer a man without a recognisable past. I was now the man Diana Murray had chosen to be her husband.

We visited a few old haunts during our fortnight at the Wotton Arms. At Cliff's End the Goldworthys were on holiday, but we were most warmly welcomed by the old groundsman-gardener who had always been a good friend of ours. We made a nostalgic visit to the Marlowe Theatre at Canterbury and I showed Diana the great castle of Dover, once commanded by Roger Mortimer, where I had tried to stretch the minds of my Cliff's End history class. We also attended Evensong at Canterbury Cathedral—my first visit since the Sunday when I stood "in loco parentis" for Paul Berners-Levine.

Somehow or other, Hugh and Margaret Dickinson learnt we were staying in Ockenham and one day we enjoyed a splendid lunch at Monteagle House, where young Piers Bovill was also present. Having escaped from his family's Eton plans, he had regained his self-confidence at King's School, Canterbury. It wasn't in his nature to be a conformist: and I was not surprised to be told that he had discovered in himself a genuine talent for painting. He was delighted for us to look at his recent work.

As we drove away from the Palladian frontage of Monteagle House down the mile-long drive, Diana squeezed my hand. "You must be quite a clever teacher," she said. "Margaret Dickinson told me, after lunch, about your holiday stint. They think you're great."

But we really preferred to spend our days exploring new places within walking distance of the Wotton Arms. If you live in that part of Kent where Ockenham is situated, you are constantly reminded that you are in the very centre of English history. Little lanes make unexpected detours to avoid some ancient Saxon burial-ground. The Roman invaders established their main supply base near Sandwich: the stark walls of Richborough still crown the hill, above the Stour estuary, in silent witness to the four hundred years of Roman occupation. Five hundred years later, William the Norman received free passage through the County, but only on condition that the old Kent system of land tenure was respected. So the Mortimers, sailing from Normandy with Duke William, came to possess the valley of Ockenham. When the senior branch of the family rode north-west to secure the Welsh border for the Conqueror, a junior branch stayed in Kent, marking the permanence of their settlement by building and endowing the church of St. Dunstan.

Thereafter—and Diana and I were happy to accept the story Miss Millie had told me—the Mortimers of Ockenham had little direct concern with the Marcher Lords' colourful history, until John of Gaunt's jealous hatred of the Earl Marshal, Roger Mortimer, came to embrace all who carried Mortimer's name: and so led to the death of Thomas and the ultimate tragedy in the churchyard at Ockenham.

Miss Millie had invited us to tea on the last Friday of our honeymoon: and promptly at four o'clock we reached her thatched cottage—I cannot imagine any of Millicent Taylor's pupils being late for school. The old lady conducted us through the living room I knew so well, and out to a small garden, full of sunshine, colour and the scent of roses. Tea was to be served on a lawn freshly mown, in a corner sheltered from the breeze.

Clearly, this was "an occasion" in my bride's honour; silver teapot, Crown Derby china, delicate cucumber sandwiches, home-made scones and a sponge cake.

Diana and I felt ourselves transported to some halcyon day before the 1914 war, perhaps when a younger Millicent Taylor, sitting at a similarly loaded tea-table at the Great House, had been reporting to Mrs. Mortimer-Wotton on the village school's activities and needs. History was here for the asking, for Miss Millie, though she had come to terms with the present, loved the past with an unquenchable love. And from her we received a further grounding in local history.

The Wottons, she told us, reached Ockenham in the 1530s when Henry VIII ordered the destruction of the monasteries and the seizure of their vast estates.

Earlier, the Kent Mortimers, so far as they escaped Gaunt's frightful vengeance, had left the county, some travelling to Ireland and others to the Welsh Marches: while their property had reverted to the Crown. So it remained until Henry VI gave it to the great monastic foundation of Leeds in return for the Prior's promise to offer daily prayers for the king's soul in the Royal Chantry within Leeds Castle. The gift of the pious Henry included both the land and manorial rights which included

169

the right to institute a priest to the Living of St. Dunstan. This was the property that Mr. Julian Wotton had expensively acquired from the Crown Commissioners.

Like most successful City merchants, young Mr. Wotton longed to own a place in the county. He was thought to have chosen Kent because other members of his family were already there. "Believe it or not," said Miss Millie, "one of them simultaneously held the Deaneries of Canterbury and York."

One thing, however, was certain. Julian Wotton knew nothing about the land. So he shrewdly reappointed the priest, John Frebody, to the Living of St. Dunstan's and continued to employ him, as the Prior of Leeds had done, as Factor responsible for the farming of the estate. Frebody was evidently a strong as well as an attractive character—there's a delightful miniature of him up at the Great House. But he boldly married a girl from Leeds village, having no more belief than Cranmer in a celibate priesthood. This secret marriage may have been the reason why the Prior sent him away from the Priory.

Much less is known about Julian

Wotton. He was a member of the Drapers' Company in the City of London: and often travelled to Antwerp to do business with the clothiers in that great city. But he certainly planned the new Manor House. Today the only relic from the great days of the Mortimers is the moat which surrounds the rose garden. But there is one other link with the previous owners. The Canterbury builder whom Julian Wotton employed on his manor house project is known to have been a direct descendant of the great Henry Yvele who redesigned the church for Lady Edwina Mortimer.

"So much for the facts," Miss Millie concluded. "But many legends persist. Some say that Sir Thomas More visited the house—he had an estate in Kent, you know." But Miss Millie doubted this tale, for, as she said, More was by this time in deep trouble with the king. "The great man probably came secretly to Ockenham to warn John Frebody who, through friends at Aldington, had become implicated in the strange affair of the Holy Maid of Kent, which eventually rebounded on More himself. But that's another story," said Miss Millie firmly. "As for the Wottons, they have continued ever since the days of Henry VIII to serve the king and farm the land, here in Ockenham. It was only a chance wedding to an Irish bride in the eighteenth century that brought the name of Mortimer back to the land the Mortimers had won for themselves at the time of the Conquest."

Miss Millie rose. I almost expected her to say, "Well, that's all for today," as if dismissing two promising students after a private tutorial. But in fact she spoke very differently and with real affection.

"Goodbye, my dears," she said. "I'm sure I've rambled on too long. But you have been very patient listeners and I've loved to have young people to talk to." She smiled at us as we thanked her—once again I had the feeling that she could be a marvellous substitute for the grandmothers I'd never known. And then she added,

"It's really for me to thank you. You see, the history books cut out the little local things that go to form a village's tradition. The text books have to be rewritten and rewritten as Empires shrink and the world gets smaller until, in a European context, we are expected to change our views on half our national heroes. So I think it's time for my storehouse of local knowledge to be passed to the rising generation while I still remember it. Actually," and there was a twinkle in her eye, "I found the children at the village school were more interested in the history of Ockenham, than in the history of England."

"You bet they were," I said to Diana as we walked away past the line of cottages that constitute the hamlet of Little Ockenham. "Lucky children to be blessed with such a teacher."

On the final Sunday of our honeymoon, we changed our plans, for Diana was determined to return to Wapping via Leeds Castle.

Before leaving Ockenham, we took Communion at St. Dunstan's, looking down from the Communion rail on the exquisite brass memorials to Lady Edwina Mortimer and her son: both of us conscious, in a mysterious way, of the company of witnesses surrounding us. Then, down the double line of yew trees which stretch from the south door, we emerged into the sunlight.

After a Continental breakfast in our rooms, we paid our account to Ted Baker, and armed with one of Luisa's Italian-style hampers, took to the Maidstone road. As we left, Michael Baker, the cheeky lad who had confused me earlier with his Italian message from *La Nonna*, dashed forward and with an irrepressible flow of his mother's native language, thrust a little bunch of roses into Diana's hand.

"How lovely," she said to him: and then to me, "Aren't they beautiful? Only an Italian would have thought of it."

"Only an Italian?" I said. "Don't make me jealous." And we laughed as we drove away.

Diana was a good driver, and often drove the Morris: but on this occasion I was at the wheel as we moved towards Leeds, with Diana doing most of the talking.

"You're very quiet, Richard," she started. "You don't mind going back via Leeds, do you?"

"No, it's a lovely idea, darling."

"But you're worried in some way."

"It's only that the last time I was there it was with my mother and . . . Leeds does things to you."

"Don't be so ridiculous. I intend to have our packed lunch at the spot where you and your mother first planned your Mortimer journey. If there are any ghosts to be laid, we'll do the deed today. And if Nicholas Maidstone peeps out from behind the beeches, I'll expect you to introduce me to him."

A very practical girl, Diana: and just as interested as I was in Miss Millie's revelations. I imagine she was unhappy that she had no personal contact with Nicholas. Still, when she reached the little rise of land above the water meadows and looked down on the peerless outline of the castle and gloriette below us, she was filled with wonder.

"It's marvellous," she said. "I've never seen such beauty in a building. You can hardly help filling it with kings and queens, bishops and abbots, and courtiers, tapestry, heralds and things . . ."

Half the afternoon we lay close together in the sunshine. London and modern living seemed far away from the English scene before us. In a sense we were much nearer to those who had lived and loved in this castle lying below us. Lazily, I leafed through the guide book spilling out the names: the Crêvecoeurs who also founded the nearby Augustinian priory; Edward I and his beautiful Eleanor of Castile; Edward III who used Henry Yvele to improve the structure; Richard II and Anne of Bohemia. It certainly was a castle fit for a queen to command. In their turn Henry IV's Joan of Navarre and Henry V's Catharine of Valois lived here; and it was here that Catherine fell in love with Owen Tudor. Could any castle be more charming or discreet for a royal romance?

I thought Diana was asleep. But she broke in, laughing. "No sign of Nicholas today?" she said. "Perhaps he's back at the Priory."

"No," I said. "He's not here today." But, catching her mood, I added, "This guide book has moved forward a hundred years and I'm told there's trouble in the royal kitchens over at the castle. A maid has given birth to a baby boy and for want of better ideas, they are calling him John Frebody."

"Try that one on Miss Millie," she laughed. "You can't fool me with your make-up stories. Come on. It's time to return to the present."

And so we drove back to London, back to reality and a council flat in Stepney. Like others who have enjoyed a perfect honeymoon, we had no doubts about the future.

6

NEXT morning I reported for duty at the Club. My primary task, it seemed, was concerned with the Mission's finances: but John also asked me to prepare some talks for various age groups that met under the Club's auspices.

"History's your subject," he said. "So let it rip. But stick to subjects that interest my clients, won't you?"

I asked for a little light and leading.

"Why, it's simple," he continued, "dead easy. You concentrate on local history and the landmarks with which the boys are familiar: the story of the river, the old dockland churches, the building of Wapping Old Stairs and St. Katharine's Dock, a few choice episodes from the Tower of London story—that's the sort of thing that will interest them.

"Or trace the early Trade Union struggle for recognition, and the sweated-labour strike of the match-factory girls—the Victorians, for all their piety, had an appalling record of labour relations, you know! You might get the boys talking about some of the more unusual pub signs. Who, for instance, was old Parr of 'Old Parr's Head'? Why does the 'Marquis of Granby' turn up so frequently? And why 'The Prospect of Whitby'? Or mug up the story of old William Booth who founded the Salvation Army. The local lads gave him and his Salvationists a terrible time: but look how they respect the Army now. Attitudes *do* change, even in the East End.

"There's one other point," he added. "Never underestimate the younger lads' intelligence. You'll soon find that their minds stretch far beyond the financial possibilities of the score-draws, and the chances of West Ham and Orient in the Cup."

John Spencer certainly knew his "clients". By and large, they were the more intelligent and serious members of the Wapping community. I was surprised how easily I held their interest once I got to know them as individuals. Perhaps the days at Cliff's End had not been entirely wasted. I remember being absurdly pleased when one of them shouted "'Ullo, Mr. Eveleigh" as I walked down Cable Street.

But it needed a saint to direct the Club's affairs, for it was fraught with disappointments. John Spencer put it to Diana and me one evening when he came round to our flat for coffee and sandwiches.

"The problem is that all the best chaps, and the girls too, abandon the place as they get educated and win advancement. They emigrate to the new housing estates in Essex, and we're left with the layabouts."

"You're looking mighty well on it," I said.

"Am I?" said John. "It's good of you to say so. I'm lucky really. Many people join us as a social penance—working out a sort of guilt complex, I suppose. That's honest and good: but often they cannot take the strain, especially when their motives are misunderstood. If there's one thing the people down here can't take, it's the condescension of the rich.

"It's easier for a parson. They reckon he's here for keeps—part of the scene, so to speak. Disappointment, real though it is, holds a different dimension for an ordained priest. Unlike your businessmen and even your schoolmasters, all of us are trained in the knowledge that our work will not be measured by success or failure: but by the continuing strength of the faith which first inspired us to enter the Ministry.

"Paul wasn't the only man, you know, to walk the Damascus road. Others have been confronted with the same vision— sometimes the most unlikely people in the most unlikely places.

"Take my case," he continued. "For me it happened in an Army cinema in Germany when the staff of Montgomery's 21 Army Group was permitted to see the film of the Belsen concentration camp. It was made, you know, on the day the British troops entered that ghastly man-made Hell. That night, on twentieth-century film, I saw the face of Christ as clearly as Paul did on the Damascus road. I saw Him in the face of a pitiful, emaciated Jew, scarcely able to walk, more animal than human, the spectre of a man expecting death, with a mind bereft of hope. So far as I know, no other man among those horrified viewers saw the eyes of Christ in the face of the dying Jew. Perhaps they were only directed at me. All I know is that they helped me to test the truth of Cranmer's prayer to a God 'whose service is perfect freedom'. Win or lose, I have no regrets at leaving Lincoln's Inn in favour of Wapping."

A few months later, I was clearing up the office after a long conference with our accountants and our Appeals Secretary when John Spencer looked in.

"Richard," he said, "can you do something for me? I've properly bricked it—arranged a vital meeting this afternoon with our architects in Bloomsbury—and clean forgotten Hannah Massey's eightieth birthday. You've heard of Aunt Hannah, haven't you? A marvellous old lady who has done a lot for the Club in her time. I'd ask Susie to come to my aid, but she's involved in some 'do' at the children's school. I'm afraid the old lady will be very disappointed if nobody from the Club makes a personal call."

So I found myself, that same afternoon, climbing three flights of concrete stairs to visit old Hannah Massey—Aunt Hannah as she was called—on the top floor of a housing development a few minutes' walk from the Club. I was armed with a bag of fruit, some flowers and a greetings card signed by John and Susie Spencer and their children. I felt absurdly nervous as I climbed the last flight. I felt certain I should be a terrible disappointment to the eighty-year-old Hannah. She was sure to regard me as a very poor substitute for her old-time friends.

However, after a long wait, the old lady shuffled to the door in carpet slippers, asked me my business with the chain still on the lock and, after a careful inspection of the Spencers' card, admitted me to her sitting room.

To my surprise, the room was spotlessly clean. There was no hint of that old-age smell which I had anticipated. And Aunt Hannah insisted that I stay to share her tea and birthday cake. "Made by my granddaughter," she said, "who is a nurse at the London Hospital, and delivered this morning by the kind lady on the ground floor. People are so good to me, Mr. Eveleigh."

Soon Aunt Hannah was telling me her life story: lady's maid at a big house in Essex, married to the head gardener and living at the Lodge; three children, two girls and a boy; boy killed in Italy at the

Salerno landings, girls married and living a long way from London; after the war, the big house sold for building land, being too big for the family to keep up; husband dead; and old Hannah left alone with her pension and a small annuity from the family she and her gardener husband had served for so long.

The story could be duplicated in many corners of post-war England. The wonderful thing about old Hannah Massey was that she refused to complain either of her luck or loneliness. While she boiled the kettle, I took a quick look round the room. The photographs on the wall confirmed her story, with "Dad" and "the boy" in places of honour. The pot plants on the window-sill were well cared for—a tribute to Mr. Massey's memory. Beside Hannah's chair I noticed some embroidery work, a well-worn Bible and a portable radio.

When she reappeared with the tea, she said,

"I know what you're thinking, Mr. Eveleigh: that an old lady who lives up here on the top floor must be very lonely. But I don't see it that way. I have my radio and my memories. And a visit like yours provides me with a surprise blessing, like a letter you haven't expected."

Even on this first visit, it was clear that Aunt Hannah's health was failing. Subsequently, I continued to visit her once a week at the same time every Thursday— she was a very orderly person. It was in the course of these visits that I discovered she possessed in her old age the same serenity —or should I say stability?—I had noticed in Miss Millie and in the Italian grandmother at the Wotton Arms. Diana, who sometimes accompanied me on these visits, had the same impression. It did something for us, perhaps because of its contrast with the endless complaints from so many of the new flat-dwellers in the Club's neighbourhood.

In the last few weeks of Hannah's life we shared a rota with "the London Hospital granddaughter" and "the lady downstairs". She died following a slight heart attack: and by chance Diana and I were on duty when she died. Her last hours were very peaceful. Her last conscious act was to guide my hand to her Bible. We both heard her slow whispered words:

"It's for you, dear boy . . . with my love

. . . for both of you . . . for today and tomorrow." She died a few minutes later, still with her hand in mine. It was the first time Diana and I had been in the presence of death.

That same evening we opened Hannah's Bible. A birthday card from the granddaughter, of whom she was so proud, had been inserted as a marker at the ninetieth Psalm. I began to read.

Lord, thou hast been our dwelling-place in all generations . . . a thousand years in thy sight are but as yesterday.

Teach us to number our days that we may apply our hearts unto wisdom . . .

O satisfy us early with Thy mercy: that we may rejoice and be glad all our days.

And let the beauty of the Lord our God be upon us.

My voice trailed away into silence. Diana said,

"You grew very fond of old Hannah, didn't you?"

"Yes," I replied. "I found it easy to love her. I'm sure the beauty of the Lord was upon her." And at that point my mind went off at a tangent. "How would she have fared, I wonder, if brave men like Wycliff and Tyndale had never lived? I suppose God always needs such people if His light is to shine in the world's darkness. It's as if God can't act without their help."

Diana looked at me, all questions in her eyes. "Darling, you do have some funny ideas," she said.

It was then that I told her of my midnight walk at Oxford at the end of the motoring holiday with my mother. It was an experience I had always kept to myself. Now the memory came flooding back to me. I began to quote the words I'd heard Wycliff use to his students.

"The Lord's words are for everyone. Before I die, the Scriptures will be available in English so that every shepherd in the land may hear Christ's words in the English language."

I felt terribly self-conscious. I knew I was blushing. My voice was uncertain—a sort of catch in my throat.

"I'm so sorry, darling," I stammered. "This experience I had in Oxford—it was a very private thing. Somehow, old Hannah reminded me of it. I've never told anyone about it before."

Diana edged closer to me and held my hand. She kissed me very gently on the forehead.

"Thank you for telling me," she said. "I'm glad you did. And now I'll tell you another private thing—only it won't stay hidden much longer. I saw the doctor this week and he confirms I'm going to have a baby—our baby. And though I said nothing to old Hannah, I'm certain as I'm sitting here that, a few days before she died, she knew that I was carrying a child."

7

FIVE months before the baby was due, Diana and I returned to Ockenham. A week's holiday at the Wotton Arms seemed the right way to celebrate our good fortune, for we had married in the knowledge that we wanted to raise a family.

In the life we had chosen for ourselves, we experienced none of the anxieties of our friends in the Home Counties whose life-style often forces them to choose between children and the first mortgage payments. In our rented flat in Stepney we were as poor as our neighbours. Like them, we accepted that a baby was a very good reason for getting married.

On our arrival at Ockenham, we received a splendid welcome from Ted and Luisa and the Baker children. In the bar and restaurant on our first Saturday night we really felt ourselves part of the company. "The Wotton" had, so to speak, become our "local".

But early next morning Ockenham's single street was deserted as we walked towards the parish church for the eight o'clock Communion service. We entered St. Dunstan's and moved through the nave to the chancel where the service was to be held. There, among the handful of people seated in the choir stalls, we noticed Miss Millie and, beside her, the unmistakable figure of Major Mortimer-Wotton.

The door from the vestry closed with a resounding creak and soon the priest's voice brought to our ears the familiar words of the liturgy. Cranmer's incomparable English suffused the little congregation.

Almighty God, unto whom all hearts are opened, all desires known and from whom no secrets are hid, cleanse the thoughts of our hearts by the inspiration of Thy holy Spirit that we may perfectly love thee and worthily magnify Thy holy name.

The past and present were interlocked. Each of us, I suppose, was engaged in some sort of communion with the God in whose honour this lovely church had been built.

Into my mind, at that moment, came a great certainty that the old master-builders of Canterbury were making it easier for each new generation to "magnify God's holy name".

But were my thoughts only known to God? Or were they also being transmitted by his grace to the girl kneeling beside me? They say this process of thought transference often happens between two people in love. What is indubitable is that after the service, as we left the church, Diana paused to read the list of previous incumbents and said in the most inconsequential way,

"John Frebody, 1521 to 1561. Your baby from Leeds Castle, Richard, must have been a born survivor."

Diana was right. Forty adult years was a long innings in the sixteenth century. This contemporary of Cranmer must have seen his way through four reigns and Heaven knows how much persecution.

"He must have seen a thing or two in his time," I agreed. "More and Fisher beheaded on Tower Hill. William Tyndale hanged and burnt as a heretic in the Low Countries . . . the Holy Maid of Kent dragged to the gallows at Tyburn . . . even

191

Henry VIII's yes-man, Thomas Cranmer, redeeming his soul as one of the Oxford martyrs . . ."

Diana interrupted. "Hey, wait a minute. I was thinking about a vicar of Ockenham, not asking for a sixteenth-century casualty list."

"Sorry," I said. "Just following a line of thought. Frebody, do you remember? The man Miss Millie linked with the Holy Maid of Kent. I believe he must have been the priest carrying the girl that I saw in my churchyard dream. I wonder if Miss Millie can explain how he managed to survive."

Two days later, we were invited to take tea with Miss Millie; a set-piece meal beautifully presented as before, but on this occasion served in the cottage living room.

"So you want to know more about John Frebody?" the old lady began. "Well, I've told you the facts: the only certain additional fact is that his miniature which I've seen at the Great House was painted in Antwerp. And why, you may ask, should an Ockenham priest visit Antwerp? My theory is that he felt safer there than in the Canterbury neighbourhood. It strengthens the legend that Sir Thomas More made a secret visit to Ockenham to warn the young priest that his life was in danger because of his association with the Holy Maid of Kent. If that was so, John Frebody would have been wise to take ship at Dover to escape the questions which might be put to him, probably under torture, by the king's secret service or the Macchiavellian Thomas Cromwell. And what more natural than a journey to Antwerp where Julian Wotton was well known to the clothiers at the so-called 'English House'?"

The old lady paused, as she had done on an earlier occasion, as if to assure herself of our interest. Then she continued.

"You're not sure, are you, about the Holy Maid of Kent? Well, I'll tell you. She was a simple country girl, called Elizabeth Barton, who worked at a farm over Aldington way—say twenty miles from here. Occasionally she fell into a trance; doctors today would probably diagnose some form of epilepsy. When in this state, she uttered prophecies in a strange, unnatural voice which greatly excited the superstitious people of Tudor England. It is said that over three thousand men and women from this part of Kent flocked to the Virgin's shrine at Court-at-Street to witness the strange phenomenon of this young girl and her trance-impelled 'voices'.

"Sadly, she was 'taken up' by some learned Benedictines at Canterbury who were opposed to Henry VIII's divorce and his break with Rome. She was persuaded to enter a Nunnery, where she was said to have 'prophesied' against the king. And although the Holy Maid, as she was now called, made public recantation of her words both at St. Paul's Cross and at Canterbury, she remained the pivot of a clerical conspiracy against the king.

"Her tragic life ended when, in the company of other priests loyal to the old order, she was condemned by Bill of Attainder to a traitor's death at Tyburn. Through all the vile Tudor ritual of public execution, this country girl's courage never wavered. Whatever value you place on the prophecies of Elizabeth Barton, her total innocence must give her a place among the martyrs of the sixteenth century.

"So much is history. The link with John Frebody is quite unproven. But he could well have been present at the little chapel of

Court-at-Street with other Ockenham folk. And it may be significant that the Great House miniature depicts him as a member of the Order of St. John of Jerusalem."

"But why significant?" we asked together.

"Well, you see, the Hospitallers at their English headquarters in the City of London were traditionally allowed, as an act of mercy, to bury the earthly remains of the poor wretches who were dragged to execution at Tyburn. And theirs was the only religious Order whose status was never challenged and its property never forfeit to the king. It's my belief that John Frebody returned from Antwerp disguised as a member of the Order: and was present at Tyburn on that grim day when Elizabeth Barton was executed. He may even have made the journey with the help of William Tyndale who was living in Antwerp at the time and busy smuggling his newly-printed Bibles into England.

"Afterwards, with the chief conspirators dead, the lesser people on Thomas Cromwell's list of suspects would have escaped further harrassment, probably with the aid of a hefty fine paid into the Royal Exchequer."

Miss Millie looked at us: the triumph of a successful research student was in her eyes. "You can make what you like, my dears, out of my old woman's tales: but you will at least know that Ockenham is not without history. You may even find that history is still being made in this village, even though it is isolated from the greater world to which the papers devote their headlines."

We left soon after the conclusion of Miss Millie's "history lesson", but somehow the story stayed with us. On the last day of our holiday, Diana and I motored over to Court-at-Street, and in a farmer's field discovered the ruins of the chapel where people had first heard Elizabeth Barton's miraculous utterances.

Seated on the bluff on which the chapel is sited and looking across the low-lying land towards Hythe and the English Channel, we could easily picture the crowd assembling on the hillside, as groups of people converged from Ashford and Rye and Tenterden and jostled for the best vantage points from which to see the promised miracles. Some would go away believing in the Maid's holy inspiration. Others, unconvinced, would return to their homes, content to report to their family on the size of the crowd. And a few scheming men would plan to use the Maid's utterances as divine sanction for their own unholy plots against the king's majesty.

Yes, it was easy enough to picture the past: but far harder to find any link between these legends and our own twentieth-century lives. Why, I kept thinking, did these people of Ockenham continue to cross my path? First Nicholas Maidstone, the Mortimers' fourteenth-century servant, sacrificing his young life in the Ockenham churchyard. Now John Frebody, one hundred and fifty years later, living no less dangerously: but by God's mercy surviving into old age. Both of them priests of Ockenham: both starting life at Leeds and owing their early survival to the monks' care for them: both of them . . . the parallel suddenly hit me between the eyes . . . both of them born out of wedlock.

I felt a need for exercise. So Diana drove the car back to Ockenham, dropping me *en route* on the edge of Lyminge forest. Armed with a one-inch Ordance Survey map, I planned to walk the last few miles along the footpaths and lanes which criss-cross the beautiful stretch of country over-looked by Chartham Down.

It was only after leaving the car that I realised I was covering the same tracks that John Frebody would have taken on his journey to Aldington and Court-at-Street. Suddenly I had the illusion that I was not alone. I received the same sensation of companionship that I had experienced on my Christmas walk, years earlier, in the valley of Ockenham.

Then it had been the voice of Nicholas Maidstone urging me forward to London —to leave the enclosed life of a private school and discover how other people lived. His prompting had taken me first to the money-making world of Monty Berners-Levine: and then to the poor but rewarding world of John Spencer and the young hope-fuls of Wapping. It had enabled me to witness in Hannah Massey and Miss Millie and even in *La Nonna* the serenity of old age. It had led me to find Diana and the shared hope of children in the days ahead . . .

But this catalogue of events since leaving Cliff's End was no more, I thought, than a series of coincidences: things that had happened to me, Richard Eveleigh—experiences thrust upon me, events I had not controlled. Or were they, I wondered, a mirrored reflection of the life of Nicholas Maidstone, who, until his final sacrifice, had travelled and acted only as the Mortimers commanded?

Now, as I emerged from a field path onto the Chartham road, I seemed to be receiving a more urgent command, firmer and altogether decisive. It had to be the voice of John Frebody . . . "You are one of us, one of us. Stop sitting on the fence."

That night, at the Wotton, Diana and I were marvellously happy. Next day she fell in with my suggestion that we return to Stepney by the old roads that John Frebody might have taken in the reverse direction after leaving the terrible scene at Tyburn. A priest anxious to avoid recognition would certainly take refuge each night at the religious houses on his route: and so Diana and I travelled via Faversham, Chatham and Dartford until we crossed the Thames at a new London Bridge. Its clear twentieth-century lines left no place for the pitch-black, ghoulish memorials which had once warned all honest citizens of the fate awaiting any man or woman who disturbed the king's peace.

We turned eastward. The past was behind us now. Passing the Tower of London we saw no sign of ravens black in mourning for the headsman's victims: and soon we emerged into the Highway and the down-to-earth sanity of East London.

Diana said,

"I know perfectly well, darling, why you chose this slow, busy, petrol-laden route to London—you've got this John Frebody on your mind, haven't you?" I smiled at her, and she continued. "Well, I think John has a lot in common with Nicholas. I know you say that one was murdered while still a young man, and the other survived into old age. But you see what I mean? They are both priests. They both serve the same little community and share the same sense of loyalty and devotion. They both keep in step with the great reformers of their day. They understand the compulsion of change. And the background music too, Richard . . . the people as well as the places . . . the sinners as well as the saints. You can hear the grief and despair of these poor people echoing down the years, crying for a leader to champion their cause. Yet the dragon they fight wins again and again. It seems as if greed is always the natural offspring of wealth and power. If each generation seeks these things above all else, the dragon won't die, will he? I mean, St. George never wins in real life."

It was a long speech to which I gave no answer. I stared through the windscreen of the Morris at the desolation of half-finished high-rise flats which represented the East End scene in 1960. I suppose it was good to know that somewhere, somebody was repairing the damage these Londoners had suffered in the power-game of war. At least, you could not personalise the greedy men of your own country as easily as in the days of John of Gaunt or Henry VIII. But would bricks and concrete break down the cumulative resentment of the powerless poor? What a hope!

Diana must have read my thoughts. She said,

"I don't believe governments provide an answer—not even good governments, not even good schools. Maybe Nicholas Maidstone and John Frebody point the better way. I reckon they did well to get out of the mainstream of political power and return to their local community."

Still, I remained silent, concentrating on the road ahead.

Diana continued her monologue. "You might say the same of John Spencer. I bet he could have been rich and powerful if he'd wanted to be: a business tycoon, perhaps, a private banker or even a Prime Minister. But he has deliberately chosen to live down here and help a few people in his immediate neighbourhood to discover a purpose in life. I think he knows what he is doing."

We turned off the Highway and into the forecourt of our block of flats—they seemed a mighty long way from Ockenham. We pulled up in front of the communal entrance and some children waved a greeting to us. Mrs. Choudhuri and the younger members of her Bengali family peeped shyly from behind the curtains of their ground floor flat, noting the time of our arrival. We used to think she kept a timetable of everybody's comings and goings.

Suddenly, I turned to Diana in the front seat of the stationary car, my mind made up. I said,

"Do you think you could bear to be a parson's wife?" She looked at me, smiled, and squeezed my hand.

"That's a very serious proposal," she replied. "But if you can make it, I reckon I can." She opened the passenger door with decision. "Let's give it a go," she said.

Part Three

THE REALITY

A people without history
Is not redeemed from time, for history
   is a pattern
Of timeless moments. So, while the
   light fails
On a winter's afternoon, in a secluded
   chapel
History is now and England.

T. S. ELIOT

1

THE die was cast. I entertained no shadow of doubt as to where I wished to go. Only some higher authority could now obstruct my determination to become an Anglican priest. I realised, as did Diana, that my hopes sprang from some sort of gut reaction—an emotional urge that was independent of reason. Yet at some time, I knew, reason would need to be harnessed to desire.

When in this kind of mood, memory plays the strangest tricks with a man. For my part, I began to repeat, parrot-wise, the subject of a long-forgotten school essay. "Emotion is the ultimate driving force in human affairs and Intelligence is only the mechanism. Discuss David Hume's Dictum—write on one side of the paper only!"

Where, I argued, was the need for discussion? Diana, who meant so much to me, was backing my decision: indeed, it could have been her prompting that finally

207

urged me forward. But reason demanded some logical explanation why indecisive, uncertain Richard Eveleigh had ended a week's holiday by throwing his cap over the windmill.

I went for a walk in Victoria Park, that vast expanse of turf which is our East End under-used equivalent to the greener grass of the Royal Parks. For hours I walked alone. When and where, I kept asking myself, had the seed been sown? How long had decision been germinating? Whence had hope sprung?

My mind travelled backwards—travelled the full extent of my life. As far back as Margaret Jones, my unknown mother, and my nameless father. Back to the mother I knew, who had given to an illegitimate child home and education: and who had died before I had given her adequate thanks for her goodness to me. My guilt lay heavily on me. I recalled the pagan honesty of Mary Winter (where was she now?) and the reliability of Harold Goldworthy: the insight and sympathy of Rosie Ashcroft when I told her of my adoptive mother's confession after her visit to Ockenham. More recently, I had observed, as wholly admirable, the obstinate courage of the European exiles, Fred and Trudi Binder: and the serenity of Miss Millie and Aunt Hannah who had each, in old age, shown me the secret of living. In all the storage of memory I could establish only one link connecting these splendid people. Each had given me something . . . my response was overdue. I had a debt to repay.

Reason was breaking in. I paused for a moment and sat on a wooden seat not yet vandalised, my feet making patterns in the dust. Yes, that was it . . . I had received so much. But what had I given in return? Defending Counsel spoke of a few years of teaching, mentioning with pride which I hope can be pardoned the cases of the Berners-Levine boys and the Hon. Piers Bovill and the lads of Wapping. He hoped a year's service at John Spencer's Club might count in my favour . . .

Stop. Hold a minute. John Spencer was no more than the last link in a chain of coincidental events which had to include my time at Number 84, the mockery of Daniel Berners-Levine and, through Daniel, my reunion with Diana . . .

I got up to resume my walk, my thoughts

focusing on the happiness Diana had brought to me and on the baby she would bear. There, surely, I could see the thread of life extending into the limitless future.

But the past was pressing upon me too: here in Victoria Park I was aware of the timelessness of God in history. Was it only chance that led me to the churchyard at Ockenham, and projected my imagination back into the past? Into the fourteenth century of the Mortimers, face to face with their faithful servant, Nicholas Maidstone? Or later, in company with Diana, into the Tudor world of Julian Wotton and his masterful priest, John Frebody? Had I, through their ghostly presence, been given inside knowledge of two revolutions in thought which had caused the people of these islands to be named "the people of the Book"? I could see the history of those days so clearly: the first forward leap towards the light, frustrated by selfish men jealous of their privilege and property: and then the second more successful leap, engineered by equally unscrupulous men who on this occasion saw in it a chance to secure the royal favour and their own advancement.

And where did Richard Eveleigh stand? With Wycliff or John of Gaunt? With William Tyndale or Henry VIII? The victory, I concluded, did not rest with the winning or keeping of a crown. The prize was a book which scholars had translated —a book which old Hannah Massey had bequeathed on her death-bed to me and Diana. A book which was to be found in every parish of our land, not least in the parish church which the Mortimers and the Wottons had raised and beautified to the glory of God.

I returned light-footed to our high-rise flat in Stepney, and ascended the stairs in the certainty that Richard Eveleigh's course had been set for him. Somewhere on the road—perhaps on a midnight encounter in Oxford or perhaps on the chancel steps at St. Dunstan—God had intervened and seed had been sown. I prayed that it had been scattered on good ground.

I had many talks with John Spencer before we were certain that it was right to seek ordination as a full-time priest of the Church of England. I told him everything about myself, burdening him with the muddled thoughts that had crossed and recrossed my mind in Victoria Park. He listened most patiently until one day he said, "I have heard all I need to hear, Richard. Go in peace, my son: and may God be with you on your journey."

Sponsored by the Bishop of Stepney, I presented myself to some very impressive clergymen at St. Albans. That was a three-day session—very relaxed, very friendly: but all the time confidence drained out of me. Never, I swear, has an examinee waited for an answer with greater anxiety.

Still, these kindly inquisitors accepted me: and that autumn I was admitted as a student at Oakhill College. Before my application was made, I was required to name three outside sponsors: and to my great delight, Diana's father agreed to join Miss Millie and Rosie Ashcroft in this capacity. It seemed to us that these three represented the different sides of my life: and would have a sympathetic understanding of the strain my period of training would be imposing on Diana. We called them collectively "The Eveleigh Supporters' Club".

For three years, I read and studied with

a concentration of effort such as I have never before applied to anything in my life. The Old and New Testaments, Doctrine, Worship, Ethics, Pastoral Studies—all had to be covered: and like every student I received practical training in taking services and preaching, as well as "parish placement" in inner-city and country parishes.

Just before Christmas in the first year of my course, our first child—a boy we called Nicholas—was safely delivered: and six months later, Diana and the baby were allowed to join me in the College. This move enabled her to attend lectures and meet the other students, some of them straight from university, others like me with varied experience in business and teaching.

Throughout the course, we wrote regularly to my Sponsors; and they were all present with Diana and the Spencers when I was ordained Deacon in Advent, 1963.

Looking back on those years of concentrated study, I doubt if any other profession or business trains its apprentices more rigorously than the Church of England. I still remember with gratitude the wisdom and understanding of those who conducted our courses, and their involvement in each candidate's personal problems. Equally, I recall the diverse talents of my fellow-students. Together, we developed a sense of purpose and companionship which grew throughout the years of our training—a purpose that was certainly shared by the wives of the three married men on the course. Despite the variety of age, intelligence and experience we were, so to speak, united in believing that we were being equipped for a great and exciting adventure.

Not that there was anything adventurous about my first appointment to a busy, prosperous parish in the Blackheath part of the Southwark diocese. The vicar had a lot going for him—much help from a growing congregation and no great poverty within the parish.

Yet there remained the constant, inevitable problems which every vicar has to face, whatever society he works in. This man, Trevor Browning, used to call them his "out of school" problems: that is to say, the problems the clergy face most days of the week without the congregation's knowledge or participation.

Generally, they start with a telephone call. Sometimes the speaker reports some sudden, unexpected tragedy like a road death or a suicide: I remember especially the case of a brilliant girl medical student gassing herself just before her finals. Sometimes the caller's anxiety is almost ludicrous: "Johnny's not happy at school, Vicar. Can you have a word with the headmaster? I can't get any sense out of him." Sometimes, the case can be remedied by careful intervention: a marriage break-up for no good reason, or a parishioner's teenage child, caught by the police in some pad in Kensington with cannabis stinking the place out.

Trevor Browning used to analyse these problems with me, always relating them to the people involved. "Applied Christianity" he used to call it. He had an uncanny skill in knowing when his caller was telling him less than the whole truth—and why. I concluded that in many localities a parson is the most important—sometimes, the only—effective social worker. His operations are secret and unpublicised, while his organisation is often limited to a single assistant in the person of his wife. In Blackheath Joanna Browning's sympathetic eyes and ears were of the highest quality. The help she gave Trevor was beyond calculation: and sometimes I used to wonder how a celibate priest could operate effectively in a parish of this type.

When Diana and I joined the Brownings at Blackheath, they were about fifty years old. Their three children were off their hands: their daughter a trained nurse married to a Sheffield doctor, one son studying agriculture and determined to get out to Central Africa on some CMS sponsored scheme, and the second boy articled to a City solicitor. Trevor and Joanna were wonderfully kind to us. On the birth of a second baby—a girl we christened Philippa —they looked after young Nicholas as if he was their own grandson. And they were scrupulous in ensuring that Diana and I enjoyed regular days off duty. "Remember, Richard. You can't lead a vicar's life unless you stick to some basic 'time off' rules and ensure that the parish knows them too."

How we loved those "days off" in

Blackheath. With Philippa in a push-chair and Nicholas governing the pace of our walking, we would wander about Greenwich Park and among the footballers on the heath.

Climbing to the high ground beside the Wolfe memorial, we would look down on the palace in which the baby Elizabeth was born to Ann Boleyn, and conjure up the leading actors in its royal past—the flamboyant, tennis-playing king; the obsequious Cranmer; the get-rich-by-flattery courtiers; and perhaps the Friars Observant who supported the claims of the Holy Maid of Kent, walking by the river in the evening light, grimly resolved to oppose the royal marriage, whatever the cost of martyrdom.

Up on the heath we often stopped at the transport café once patronised by Piers Bovill and me on our expedition to London. From there we could share Wat Tyler's first sight of the great city and its hundred churches lining the further bank of the Thames: with Southwark in the foreground, beckoning the Tyler to the bridgehead which had to be seized if his peasant army was to reach its objective.

Blackheath was a place we both loved —full of associations, ancient and modern.

I stayed on with the Brownings after I was priested, and it was not until 1966 that I was told of a new job waiting for me.

"An East End curacy," Trevor told me, "with loads of responsibility. Up towards Bethnal Green. The Vicar, Thomas Shepherdswell, is a remarkable old man— been in that area all his working life. Lost his wife ten years ago. A bit long in the tooth now. It will be good for him and the parish to have you, Diana and the children around."

He smiled as he rattled off the job specification. "I expect you'll get more help from your friends at the Mission than from me. But you'll find that each parish in those parts has its own personality. If you want an occasional change of air or even some outside advice, Joanna and I will be here. There's not much more than the width of the Thames between us."

So it was that in the autumn of 1966 Diana and I took up residence in part of the old-fashioned vicarage of St. Mildred's

Church, E1. where the Rev. Thomas Shepherdswell had been in occupation for the past thirty years.

2

WE found the church of St. Mildred situated in one of the more neglected parts of East London, a bit to the south of the Bethnal Green Road, yet reasonably close to the City.

For some reason beyond human understanding, it was the only church for miles around to have escaped unscathed from the London Blitz. In 1966 it still stood, four-square and forbidding—a stark, depressingly ugly building, its bricks blackened with London grime and its windows protected by wire cages from the brickbats of local vandals. That virtuous Kentish princess, St. Mildred, had surely deserved something more shapely from the Victorian do-gooders who, in the 1880s, had sought to drive away the devil from East London by raising this rectangular eyesore on a corner where a row of poor houses joined a street of little retail shops. But there, for better or worse, stood St. Mildred's. There was no history in the church and none was likely to be made there.

Normally, the doors which opened directly onto the street were kept locked, though there was precious little in the church to attract the professional thief. But if you gained entry, you would discover an unadorned and under-used place of worship, with one third of the interior partitioned from the nave and used for the occasional "social". Heating was non-existent so far as I could feel, though I should add, in St. Mildred's favour, that the interior was scrupulously clean and free from dust. This small fact warmed my heart. Somebody, at least, cared for the place.

If our first sight of the church was a somewhat grim introduction to our new commitment, the vicarage was altogether more impressive. At the time of St. Mildred's foundation, an elegant Queen Anne house—a curious local survival from more spacious days—had been bought as a vicarage and, like the church it served, had also escaped both war damage and the demolition squads. It even boasted a small garden and lay back from the building line in a side street about 100 yards from the church. It would have provided ideal accommodation for a family man, but was ludicrously large for a widower without children.

Our family was to occupy that part of the house which had been used by the previous curate. We counted ourselves fortunate to possess a separate entrance, kitchen, bathroom and lavatory. Our sparse personal belongings fitted easily into the rooms appointed to us; our only domestic anxiety being a partial dependence on an antiquated central heating system which was controlled from the other half of the house.

Moving through the connecting door between our quarters and the main body of the building, one was liable to come face to face with the Rev. Thomas Shepherdswell or, more probably, his formidable housekeeper, Mrs. Eliza Jones. Even in old age the vicar's appearance was noteworthy for a shock of white hair which showed no sign of thinning. He was clean-shaven, an inveterate pipe-smoker, a mere five foot nine inches tall but remarkably vigorous for his age: in his student days he had been a boxing "blue". He still seemed to be as tough as old rope and impervious to cold (we noticed that even in the coldest weather he never wore gloves). Indeed he was apparently indifferent to all creature comforts. But we quickly discovered that he was a man of infinite wisdom, with a fantastic knowledge of those who lived in his crowded parish.

As to Eliza, she was a war widow—Mr. Jones having been blown to smithereens in the 1940 Blitz. Her grey hair, drawn back from a high forehead, added to the severity of a thin nose and a mouth which rarely smiled. Her appearance, when opening the front door of the vicarage, would have kept unwanted intruders at a distance as surely as an Alsatian guard-dog. But curiously, she had a way with children. From the very first days at St. Mildred's vicarage young Nicholas loved her, and nothing pleased her more than to be left in charge of him and Philippa.

Soon after our arrival, we learnt that Eliza's two sons had received their schooling in Somerset as war-time evacuees. That may have been the reason why they had both deserted East London as soon as they could earn a living. One was working on a farm in the West Country and the other was a "brickie" in Australia. Eliza was proud of her family. She spent her summer holidays with the farming son, and dreamed up fabulous stories of the wealth the other boy was accumulating in the suburban tentacles with which post-war Melbourne was grabbing and ruining its surrounding countryside. But she, for her part, remained wedded to the streets in which her late husband had lived and died. She now had only one mission in life—to look after "the Reverend". If that meant cleaning and catering for the church as well as the vicar, so be it. She knew, she said, her station.

This, then, was the world we were called to serve—the world of Eliza Jones and heaven knows how many others whose lives were largely confined to the streets around St. Mildred's. It might look drab at first sight, but it contained far more excitement than you would ever find in the respectable, well-ordered world of Trevor and Joanna Browning. Diana and I were stimulated by the prospect before us.

The variety was infinite, even if you excluded from the reckoning the hopeless drunks and the peripatetic criminals. The parish included, for instance, a block of pre-fab bungalows in which Punjabi was the spoken language and Asian cooking the prevailing smell. New flats were rising fast and already contained many West Indian families. Unlike the Pakistanis, the West Indians wanted to mix with their white fellow-citizens and, perhaps because of this, incurred more local resentment than the Asian community. We also held some responsibility for a church primary school, although the over-elevens attended secondary schools outside the parish boundaries.

Apart from St. Mildred's, there were few places where people could meet except in the pubs and betting shops which peppered the district. Yet there remained one universal meeting place which is common to the whole of London, and especially to that part of London east of Aldgate pump. The little shops and the street market stalls, staffed and often owned by Indians, were the focal points of contact where all the world met.

Diana and I fitted easily enough into this society which was not markedly different

225

from that of the Wapping families with whom we had worked during our time with John Spencer.

Under Tom Shepherdswell's direction, I answered many of the personal calls reaching the vicarage. As a result, I soon conquered my innate shyness about knocking on strange doors and, with equal speed, gained an exact knowledge of the local street plan.

"Always walk," was the old man's rule for curates. "Always dress like a priest—you need to be identified and you're expected to be distinctive. In this parish the parking of a car or bicycle is either impossible, or a bad commercial risk. So keep them for the day when you feel you must escape.

The old man chuckled. "Don't be alarmed, Richard. I'm only prescribing a 'keep fit' programme. Actually, doors will open to you more easily than in Blackheath: and your welcome will be warmer than in those respectable suburbs where the vicar's approach to a strange house is viewed with suspicion long before he reaches the neighbour's front gate. As for your lovely Diana, she possesses the best of all passports into the Cockney heart. Just look how Eliza dotes on Nicholas and Philippa."

Tom Shepherdswell was a wise old man. He had forgotten more about the East End than most of us would ever learn. And how right he was about making friends.

Among our earliest contacts were Jane and Steve Bloxham. The latter was a self-employed taxi-driver, still paying instalments on a new taxi which had just replaced the ancient model inherited from his father. He kept it in an old shed in a little cobbled cul-de-sac, just round the corner from his house and close to Shoreditch High Street. Jane did not go out to work, being occupied with her children and looking after her husband's business accounts. But as one of the Bloxham children was the same age as our son, Nicholas, she often met Diana at the local school when delivering or collecting children.

With new friends like Steve and Jane Bloxham to encourage us and with Tom Shepherdswell to guide us, we began to feel that within a few months we might really be of some service to the community.

But the emptiness of the church on Sundays depressed us. True, St. Mildred's enjoyed the help of a dedicated organist, a local music teacher who kept together a motley choir. But as to the congregation, we could only count on a handful of old loyalists like Eliza Jones; a Tamil-speaking family from Madras separated by language from other Asian residents; a Pakistani GP and his dentist wife; the local headmistress; and the occasional layabout seeking a little Sunday warmth before the pubs opened. The families round St. Mildred's hardly knew what the inside of their church looked like except when their children came to be baptized or married. "Somehow," as Diana put it, "we must unlock the doors."

And so we conceived the idea of staging a Friday night concert. At first, we were at a loss to know where we could find artistes who would be willing to give their services "for free" in such unglamorous and unprestigious surroundings, but a chance visit from Susie Spencer put us on course. Paul Berners-Levine, she told us, had recently brought a trio of fellow students from the Royal Academy of Music to the Mission and received a great welcome.

A call to Number 84 confirmed that Paul would be delighted to help. But—true showman that he was—he considered the evening at the Mission had lacked variety. Could we find a second piano . . . somebody who could recite or get some children singing . . . or something?

We saw what Paul meant and planned accordingly. Tom Shepherdswell gave his blessing to the enterprise, merely insisting that it was our show.

"Remember," he said, "posters are essential, and only three items matter: the place, the time and the word 'free'. The 'where' and 'why', if you get my meaning."

The signal turned to green. First we persuaded the organist to chip in with some recorder-playing children from St. Mildred's choir, and from the local school which also provided us with a second piano. Paul agreed to find a second pianist provided we guaranteed that the two pianos were tone true. Finally Diana, who had loved acting at school, consented to do her own thing. Cats, we agreed, was to be her theme. All the homes we visited loved cats. Diana would introduce them to T. S. Eliot's *Old Possum's Book of Practical Cats*.

The show was shaping up nicely.

Posters, organised by the Bloxhams, stared at us from houses, betting shops and market stalls—Friday, 15 May: 8 p.m.: refreshments. A musical evening at St. Mildred's: Entry FREE.

The day arrived, a fine evening in early summer; and the locals came streaming in. Whole families, single old ladies, unaccompanied children. There was even a back-up contingent from Number 84 in the persons of Paul's parents and Fred and Trudi Binder. By eight o'clock, there was standing-room only and children were sitting cross-legged on the floor in the apse at the front of the church. I welcomed the audience and Paul took over the show.

He was really superb as he explained what was in store. First, a Haydn Trio. Next, the recorder-playing children with a theme from Thomas Tallis. Next the curate's wife would recite a poem about somebody everybody knew. She would be followed by a surprise item—hence the two pianos standing side by side. And so to a leg-stretching interval (refreshments by courtesy of Mrs. Eliza Jones)—with a little Mozart to follow, if the audience was still there.

The boy's confidence was infectious. Standing at the back of the church, Diana and I could sense that the audience was in the right mood. Diana left me as the Trio retired to the vestry and the children lined up under the organist's direction. As Thomas Tallis took over, I felt a tap on the shoulder and a voice whispered,

"Hullo, Richard. I'm the surprise item . . . the second piano." I turned to find Rosie Ashcroft beside me.

"Yes," she said, "Paul insisted. We've been practising like crazy at Number 84. But I'm terribly nervous. Can I stay back here until the big moment?"

So Rosie and I listened together, first to the children (much parental applause), and then to Diana introducing the people of St. Mildred's to T. S. Eliot's Mystery Cat.

Macavity's a Mystery Cat: he's called the
                Hidden Paw
For he's the master criminal who can
                defy the Law.

As Macavity's mysterious disappearances multiplied the audience became completely hooked. Diana, looking truly lovely in a long, brightly coloured skirt and a white blouse with a high neck, was persuaded to follow Macavity by taking the audience on the train to Scotland with Skimbleshanks —the Cat of the Railway Train.

During the applause that followed Rosie moved up the side aisle towards the chancel where Paul was waiting for her, and a radiant Diana rejoined me, her eyes sparkling. Arm in arm we moved across to the side of the church to see whether Eliza was ready with the coffee and biscuits for the interval. One look and our happiness vanished. Eliza was not at her post. Something was wrong. A helper said, "Eliza Jones? She's gone to fetch the Reverend. She don't like what she's seen at the church door."

Sure enough, a set of young toughs were milling about at the open door onto the street: just out of the pub, I reckoned, and wondering what to do next. But what does the curate do? Keep quiet and hope for the best? It was probably fear that froze me into indecision.

Paul was already introducing the surprise item, two pianos playing some Dvořák dances.

"You'll quickly pick up the tunes and the rhythms," he said, "and if the children want to sing or sway or dance around us, Mrs. Ashcroft and I will be delighted."

With that, Rosie and Paul crashed into the opening chords of the Slavonic Dances. First the Mazurka in E Minor: then a change of rhythm to the Polonaise in B flat: and finally to a Czech peasant dance called the Sousedka.

It was a triumphant success. Given those two old upright pianos, would Brendel and Klien have done better? The children up front began to dance and the older folk were swaying to the rhythm of the music. As the final chord sounded the applause seemed sufficient to lift the roof off St. Mildred's.

Up to that point, the bully boys at the door had kept quiet, overawed perhaps by the children round the two pianos. But with Rosie leaving the stage and Paul standing alone to announce the interval, their moment had arrived. A bag of flour was accurately lobbed over the heads of the audience to burst at Paul's feet. One of the young thugs swept the plastic cups and the biscuits off the trestle tables. Angry

233

menacing voices began to chant like the Nazis we thought had been destroyed.

"Yer bloody Jew, standin' there in a Christian church. Get back to yer bleedin' ghetto. We don't want you 'ere, nor yer wog friends, nor yer lousy music . . ." Our great concert was going to end in pandemonium.

I hurried towards the door, somewhat heartened to find a furious Fred Binder at my side. But Tom Shepherdswell was there before us and had already taken command. The old warrior had arrived as if by magic, and was standing face to face with a young bruiser twice his size.

"Get out of my church," I heard him say in his low resonant voice. "I want no more nonsense from you and your bully boys. I've called the police . . . Now, get out."

The big fellow, clearly the gang leader, laughed.

"Come off it, little man. We don't take orders from the likes o' you, do we, boys?"

It was the last word he spoke that night. Tom's left fist shot out, hitting his unwary opponent in the left eye. A right-hook whipped into his chin and within seconds he and his mates backed out of the church straight into the arms of the police, who had been summoned by the old man before he had hurried over from the vicarage.

I followed the young thugs out of the church and saw them unceremoniously herded into a police van and driven away. Then I re-entered the church with a police sergeant who had taken charge of the operation.

The action had been so swift that the people in the church had little time to panic; but we were horrified by the scene that met our eyes on our return. There on the floor, a few yards from the entrance, lay Tom Shepherdswell, breathing in heavy spasms, his fine old face contorted, his collar pulled away. The Pakistani doctor from the congregation was crouched beside him, one hand on Tom's pulse, the other inside his shirt against his chest. Eliza was kneeling at his head which was resting on a low kneeler covered by her tatty old shawl. And behind them Fred Binder, assisted by Monty Berners-Levine, was holding back the crowd. Nobody could have acted more swiftly than the police sergeant. He took in the scene at a glance, and, within seconds, was calling for an ambulance on his short-wave radio. A few minutes later, with the doctor beside him, Tom was on his way to the London Hospital. And I was left to pick up the pieces.

3

FOR a fortnight the doughty old fighter clung to life in the Intensive Care Unit of the London Hospital, with no visitors permitted into his room except for the Archdeacon who was a life-long friend.

The empty study on the far side of the connecting door at the vicarage gave Diana and me a strange sense of isolation in a world we didn't fully understand: and during each of those fourteen days the old man was constantly in our thoughts.

But we were also deflated by a sense of personal failure. The plan for "Music at St. Mildred's" had gone most horribly wrong. The excitement of preparation, the success of Diana's own performance, the heady triumph of the Slavonic Dances and the honest joy of the audience in the crowded church—all wrecked and nullified by the obscenities of a few drunken louts. And when the trouble came, I, Richard Eveleigh, had frozen into inaction while our brave old vicar had cleared the hoodlums out of the church.

I could not sleep at night. My mind returned endlessly to the sequence of events which followed Tom Shepherdswell's intervention on that fatal Friday night. Formally closing the show—what else could I do? Saying goodnight like an automaton to the people filing out of the church, yet scarcely conscious of their words of sympathy. Wandering to the vestry to commiserate with Paul and his two companions and making sure that their instruments had escaped damage. Watching uselessly while Eliza Jones and the other women, aided by Diana and Rosie, philosophically cleared up the mess round the trestle table where the coffee and biscuits should have been served. Bidding farewell to Rosie and the party from Number 84: and finally, returning to the vicarage with Diana and Eliza, completely deflated.

Day by day we performed our routine duties—Diana with the children, I with the church services and the calls which continued to reach the vicarage. And every minute of the waking day, a sense of personal guilt possessed me. I knew—who did not?—that if I had not been so pathetically slow, dear old Tom would be sleeping in his own bed.

I was shaken out of this depression when the Archdeacon brought us news of Tom Shepherdswell's death. His life had come to an end quite suddenly after a further heart attack, and the Archdeacon had come straight from the hospital to tell us. The vicarage door was opened by Eliza who burst into tears even before the Archdeacon spoke. Dear, faithful Eliza, she was no stranger to death and disaster. But for her, nobody could replace "the Reverend". It was, I think, the only time I ever saw her Spartan courage at breaking-point.

For me, there was no longer time for grief or recrimination. An old man had died: and under the Archdeacon's direction I was in charge at St. Mildred's. The Press and neighbouring clergy to be informed. A service to be arranged: hymns and music, prayers and seating. All the details in my hand: the theme to be one of thanksgiving for Tom Shepherdswell's life. The Archdeacon would conduct the service and the Bishop would give the address.

For the second time in a month, St.

Mildred's was packed to overflowing. The people of the East End flocked to the church to honour the priest they had lost: and they departed, I honestly believe, with a new gratitude and pride in their hearts that such a man should have given them the totality of his life and his love. That day, the proud sorrow of Eliza Jones was shared by many East London families who honoured Tom Shepherdswell's memory.

The Archdeacon—so masterful that Diana and I always referred to him as "Grantly", though, heaven knows, Barchester had nothing in common with Stepney—thanked me after the service.

"Well done, Richard," he said. "Don't worry about the past or the future. I want you to carry on at St. Mildred's for the time being. I'm always available in a crisis and the Rural Dean and local clergy will help. We'll talk again in a few months' time when we can see the way ahead more clearly."

And so I carried on, at times encouraged and gratified to see new faces at St. Mildred's on Sundays: but always with Grantly's words "for the time being" sticking in my mind. There was, I heard on the clerical grapevine, a plan to merge

St. Mildred's with a neighbouring parish and sell the church as a community centre to the local Council. If the rumour was true, where did we go from here?

The one stabilising factor in our life at the vicarage was the continued presence of Eliza Jones. She told me she was determined to "keep her station": and I really could not argue with her, especially as we relied on her to clean the church and act as baby-sitter. You didn't argue with Eliza anyway. "The Reverend would like me to stay," she assured me confidently, "and I ask you, Mister, who's to take Nicholas to school and look after Philippa if Mrs. Eveleigh has another baby? You've got to look ahead, you know."

I reckoned Eliza's vision could see at least twelve months ahead, so for the time being she continued to live her day as she had done for the past thirty years. That is to say, she kept the church clean and the vicarage central heating going (more or less); and she cleaned the Reverend's study which she expected me to use for opening the post, if nothing else. Indeed, she treated me as if I was "the Reverend", except that she continued to address me as "Mister".

One evening, about six o'clock, when Diana was preparing the two children for bed, Eliza stumped in through the connecting door.

"It's the Bloxham boy," she announced, "'im that plays with Nicholas. Says it's real urgent, Mister: and must see you at once. 'E's waiting in the Reverend's study. Seems as if 'is secret 'as to be told be'ind closed doors." She punctuated her speech with a disapproving sniff. In Eliza's book, little boys should not be allowed to disturb the curate's leisure! But then she added more meaningfully,

"When boys came to see the Reverend and seemed out of breath like, 'e always took 'em seriously."

When Eliza broke into my "off duty" evening I was reading a novel and wearing an old tweed jacket and flannel trousers, not expecting visitors. I mention this to explain how on this occasion I failed to observe the Reverend's eleventh commandment.

"Never go out round here, Richard, unless you're dressed like a priest. A dog collar gives you a bit of protection as important as the Salvationist's uniform or the Nun's headdress. To outsiders a uniform is your best passport to respect."

But that's by the way. Responding to Eliza's firm advice, I laid Graham Greene aside and followed her to the Reverend's study to find the little Bloxham boy almost incoherent with anxiety.

"Mum says," he stuttered, "Mum says, come at once. The police have got Dad and the cab or something. She wants you quick, Mister."

It sounded like trouble—big trouble. Without further consideration I asked Eliza to tell Diana where I was going and hurried off with the boy to the Bloxham home.

I found Jane in great distress.

"Thank God you've come," she said, and raced on with her story. "Stevie decided to drive late last night. There's a lot of extra money to be 'ad from them West End fares, you know. But 'e never comes 'ome this morning. I'm worried stiff, but I go out with the kids to the shops. When I gets back about midday, there's a policeman waiting for me. Nothing to worry about, 'e says. Your 'usband's 'elping us with some inquiries. It means keeping 'im and the cab for the moment. Then 'e adds kindly enough, don't worry, dear. Your 'usband's OK. So I leave it like that. But Stevie's still not 'ome, Mister. And now look what's come through the letter box."

Jane handed me a scruffy piece of paper. The message was unsigned but the capital letters, carefully printed, were all too legible. "Tell Steve to keep his mouth shut or expect a nasty accident."

"Have you reported this to the police?" I asked.

"No, Mister," she said, "I'm scared to leave the children, so I wondered if you'd 'elp."

"Of course," I said. "Did the copper tell you which station he came from?"

"Well, 'e said as Stevie were at Clerkenwell, so I suppose 'e came from there. But I didn't really worry. You see, I thought Stevie would be 'ome by now. That is, until I got this note."

Poor Jane began to cry. I did my best to reassure her before hurrying on my way. There was no telephone, but I reckoned that by walking fast I could make Clerkenwell police station within half an hour.

There were still a lot of people in Shoreditch High Street, as I moved along Great Eastern Street at a pace which would have done John Spencer credit. I cut across the City Road south of the big traffic roundabout and entered Old Street by way of Bunhill Fields.

From this point my course was straight as the crow flies—past the exposed desolation of St. Luke's church, past some Italian and Indian restaurants, past the wholesale dress-making establishments, past the Golden Lane crossing. By now the shops were closing for the day. As I crossed Aldersgate into the Clerkenwell Road I found the pavement comparatively clear of pedestrians.

Perhaps it was this absence of people that gave me the queer feeling that I was being followed. I varied my pace, first a little faster, next a little slower. Then, as I reached St. John's Lane, I deliberately turned left and stopped just round the corner, as any tourist might do, to admire the Priory gateway of St. John of Jerusalem. For a few moments, I waited there.

It was all that remained of the Hospitallers' great mediaeval Foundation. Great Heavens, I thought, if Miss Millie's story has any truth in it this is the place where John Frebody of Ockenham must have lodged at the time of Elizabeth Barton's execution.

Somehow, the irrelevant thought gave me confidence. Laughing at my anxiety I turned back into the Clerkenwell Road and hurried through the still unrepaired dilapidation of the London Blitz. Subconsciously, I began to picture the place in its earlier days. To my left, the gateway where I had been sheltering and where John Frebody had presented himself on returning from Antwerp. To my right the Priory church, sacked by Wat Tyler, demolished by German bombs and now restored over the eleventh-century crypt on which the first church had been built. To my left again, the peace of the Charterhouse, the home of the Carthusian martyrs who followed the Holy Maid of Kent to Tyburn. And hard beside it, Smithfield where young Mortimer had stood by Richard of Bordeaux in his finest hour . . .

I pulled myself together. "Stop conjuring

246

up the past," I said to myself. "Snap out of it, Richard Eveleigh. Your concern is with a twentieth-century London taxi-driver—not with rebellious peasants or Tyburn martyrs." Instinctively, I quickened pace.

I suppose I was within half a mile of the police station when two men suddenly closed in on me and, with considerable expertise, frog-marched me into a small, inconspicuous pub called The Monk's Head. One on each side of me, they had me through the door before I realised what was happening.

"Want a word with you," the smoother of the two men began without preliminaries, after steering me to a dimly lit table well away from the bar. "Know Stevie Bloxham, don't yer? Or is it 'is Missus you're friendly with?" He spoke in a low, menacing voice. "An' what finds yer strollin' round Clerkenwell at this time of night, eh?"

I looked at the two men, the one with over-padded shoulders who did the talking, and his companion as dumb as they come, but with a fighter's fist. The pub was almost empty—just a barman and a young couple sitting at the counter. Could be a medico, I thought, out with a nurse from Barts. I stalled, playing for time.

"Sorry, but I don't know what you're talking about. Just start again, will you?"

"Don't know nothing of Stevie Bloxham?" the talking number was off again. "Don't come that crap with me, mate." He turned to his pal. "Gawd, this bloke makes me bloody thirsty. Go get us all a drink, Jimmy." The dumb fighter returned with a double whisky for his companion and two pints of bitter, one of which he pushed across to me.

The talker tried a new line. "Now we're all nice an' friendly, let's start again. We're pals of Stevie, right? An' we don't want 'im or 'is missus or 'is kids to come to any 'arm —nor 'is bleedin' cab neither, which is the pride and joy of 'is life, do we, Jimmy?" The latter nodded and downed his beer.

"So what are we talking about?"

"Just this, stranger. We don't know 'oo you are, but we don't like you stickin' yer nose in what don't concern you. And that includes what 'appened to Stevie last night. Got the message, loud and clear?"

One thing was certain. These hoodlums

were no friends of Steve Bloxham. Steve was honest and straight—I'd go bail for him anywhere. This pair of thugs were as twisted as a couple of corkscrews. If only I could get the police. But how do you act when you are totally out of communication? I realised with a very nasty feeling in the pit of the stomach that nobody knew where I was: and only Jane Bloxham knew where I was going.

I looked towards the young couple at the bar. They seemed totally absorbed in each other, though the young man's shoulders suggested he might shove his weight in a rugby scrum. I thought the barman looked pretty tough, too. He was sizing up my companions with a speculative look in his eye. I guessed he had seen them before and didn't like what he saw. I made to get up.

"Well, thanks for the tip and the beer," I said. "Have one for the road on me." The talker pulled me back.

"Not quite so fast, stranger. We don't want no trouble but we'd like your address before you go, just so we can get in touch if we want to."

He tried to hold my arm. I jerked myself-free and threw the rest of the beer in his face. The ponderous Jimmy made to get up but I landed my fist on his nose and he fell back, overturning his chair. The smooth fellow, wiping the beer off his flashy light suit, said very quietly to his mate, "Fix the little bastard, Jimmy," and that's the last thing I heard that night.

The pug doubled me up with a vicious blow to the stomach and a right hand jab at my left eye. My head cracked back onto the edge of an adjoining table. I must have been knocked out flat.

My next conscious moment came many hours later, when I found myself in a darkened hospital room with a splitting headache, and a bandage round my head. I was vaguely aware of a nurse standing over me.

"Richard?" she said, "remember?"

Remember? Good God. Of course I remembered. I was back at Cliff's End and I wasn't dreaming. Wherever I was, the voice I heard was the voice of Mary Winter. And I knew, without a shadow of doubt, that it was Mary's hand I felt resting lightly on my forehead.

4

I MUST have remained in a state of coma until the afternoon of the day following the punch-up at The Monk's Head. I could see nothing for there was a bandage covering my eyes: but the nurse's voice belonged to Mary Winter as unmistakably as the strong, capable hands which were very gently changing the dressing of the wound below my left eye. As she worked, she was speaking in short sentences without awaiting or expecting any coherent reply. It was as if I was listening to someone talking to herself.

"You're a lucky chap, Richard," I heard her say. "Surgeon reports the skull X-ray reassuring . . . confirms no permanent damage to the eye . . . wants you kept here for a few days before sounding the "all clear" . . . nothing, I'm afraid, to help your poor old headache except aspirin . . . going off duty now . . . see you in the morning."

I swallowed the aspirin she gave me and drifted into a troubled sleep. But a splitting headache made me restless. Hardly had I dozed off when a series of horrible night-mares disturbed me.

First, I found myself involved in the ghastly ritual of a Tudor execution. I could not escape from a jeering mob held back, at a short distance from the gallows, by a square of red-coated militia ... the hangman squatting like a monkey on the cross-tree, testing the rope and grimacing at the crowd ... a young country girl standing on a horse-drawn cart below him, dressed in a poor shift which gave her no protection from the cold, the noose of the rope slipped over her head. Suddenly a cry from the girl silenced the crowd—"Into thy hands, O Lord, I commend my spirit." As the dray jerked away, I woke to find the night-nurse beside me.

I must have fallen asleep again, but a new fantasy assailed my mind. I was back at St. Mildred's, only to find that our old friend, the Archdeacon, had been trans-formed into an overpowering bully—ordering me about, shouting me down when I tried to speak, riding rough-shod over the little world Diana and I had created round about St. Mildred's. He was as terrifying to me as a giant to a small child. I woke, crying with frustration, unable to protect Diana and myself . . .

The night-nurse smoothed my bed-clothes and gave me more aspirin. But as dawn broke, I was dreaming again, recapturing the yesterdays of memory. I was back at Cliff's End, back in the sun-kissed days of my first summer term at the school, bewitched by Mary Winter—the glow of her body, her fair hair, her mocking voice, the sudden initiation of love, the dangerous exciting journeys to her room . . . I fought to contain myself, feeling as guilty as an adolescent schoolboy . . .

And then, as I woke in this unfamiliar room, I was aware of Mary Winter moving about, brisk and efficient in her nurse's uniform: temperature-taking, washing me, filling up some mysterious chart, bringing me a cup of tea. She rearranged my bandage so that I could see with my right eye: and I saw she was wearing a small cross.

"When shall I see Diana?" I asked in a querulous voice I hardly recognised. "Where has she gone? Why isn't she here?"

By way of answer Mary walked across the room and returned with a vase of red roses.

"My dear Mr. Richard Eveleigh," she said, assuming the role of a stern, disapproving nurse, "your wife was with you yesterday while you were in a state of coma and she'll be back today. Meanwhile, she left these roses for you from the vicarage garden." Then she added in a very different tone of voice, "I'd say the garden behind your big house means a lot to Diana—a little patch of colour and love in a dim and over-crowded world."

Mary moved away and returned with a card from Nicholas. "Here's another present from your family. I'm not sure whether this colourful abstract indicates a latent artistic talent in your son, but there's no doubt about the sincerity of the signature surrounded by noughts and crosses."

She laughed and then became serious. "Now listen to me, Richard. You want to exercise a little patience—don't priests also have to practise what they preach? Diana will be here later in the day, as I've told you. But you're only allowed one visitor at a time, and the police have first call. They will be seeing you for ten minutes after the doctor has made his round."

"I don't care a hoot about the police or the doctor," I said angrily. "For God's sake, try and understand. What do I say to Diana? What does she know about you and me?"

Mary looked down at me—the same blue eyes, the same teasing smile.

"Just stop worrying," she said. "Yesterday, while you were still out for the count, Diana and I had plenty of time for talking: and she told me she was two months pregnant. She was also delighted to have me identified at last. Husbands and wives may be wise not to explore each other's past: but your Diana has always known about us, because that sneaky woman who followed me at Cliff's End learnt about our affair from Keith Figgis and saw fit to warn her young protégée about your wicked ways with women! Stupid creature—I guess her warning was enough to make Diana decide to find out about you for herself."

She kissed me lightly on the head above my bandage. "You're a lucky chap, Richard Eveleigh. Diana's a super girl and

255

she knows our love affair came to an end on the day I decided my vocation was nursing, not marriage. That was when I entered the Catholic Church.

"Now just relax, you old silly. Women sometimes take a few years to discover what they want to do in life. But what about men? Work it out for yourself and you'll find you took ten years to decide you wanted to be a parson."

I held her hand for a moment before she left the room. "Bless you," I said. "I'm glad you're still around."

The police were quickly satisfied with my story of what transpired before I was steered into The Monk's Head. But I also learnt from the Inspector that the young couple at the bar had been a policeman and police woman in plain clothes. They were watching the pub on the strength of a tip-off and hoping for a bigger catch. But my entry baffled them. Until the fight started, they thought I was one of the criminals. Only when I was knocked out did they move into action—evidently with commendable and decisive speed. Both assailants, the Inspector assured me, were now in custody and likely to face more serious charges than knocking a parson unconscious. In fact, they would soon be facing trial in company with a set of crooks who had robbed a sub-post-office near Heathrow and been tracked down on the strength of Steve Bloxham's evidence. We parted with congratulations and thanks on my side and best wishes for a quick recovery on theirs.

They had only been with me for fifteen minutes, but my head was splitting when Mary returned with the midday meal.

She helped me to sit up and rearranged my pillows. Then she said,

"I'm afraid you won't be seeing Diana today, Richard. A Mrs. Jones rang from the vicarage while the police were with you, and told us that the doctor wants Diana to stay in bed for a few days. It may be just a precaution, but I think there must be some danger of a miscarriage. This Mrs. Jones was very chatty. She sent you her best wishes and wanted you to know that Mrs. Spencer—have I got the name right? —had come over from Wapping to keep Diana company. Also that Nicholas and Philippa were little angels—her words, not

257

mine: and that your father-in-law might pay you a call later today."

I'd been worrying about Diana all the morning and was hardly surprised when Dr. Murray visited the hospital and confirmed that Diana had lost the baby.

"Rotten for you both," he said, "and I'm sorry not to have better news. But it's happened early in her pregnancy and there's no reason why you shouldn't add to your family when you're clear of your present troubles. The best thing you can do is to return to the vicarage as soon as the hospital will let you go. But you'll need to take life quietly for a few weeks— definitely no duties at the church. And then I would advise you to take Diana away for a holiday break, before returning to work. That's for you to say, but I'm very impressed by the competence of Eliza Jones. It was she who took charge yesterday, ringing the doctor and me and that nice Mrs. Spencer—not to mention keeping the children happy and occupied. Not many professional men have such a reliable adjutant at call."

The old doctor smiled at me as he said goodbye. "I'll stay in London," he said, "until you return to the vicarage, just in case Diana wants a little reassurance. And, anyway, I've promised to take Nicholas to the Zoo tomorrow. This wretched business has, at least, given me the chance to meet my grandchildren on their home ground."

Within forty-eight hours I was back with Diana at the vicarage. For a further fortnight my intermittent headaches continued, though the colossal bump on the back of my head disappeared and the cut under my left eye healed quickly. But I could not throw off the depression burdening my mind. I was sure it was my silly tiff at the pub that had precipitated Diana's miscarriage. And though she made a quick recovery, my feeling of sadness and the sense of loss continued as persistently as the wretched headaches which made me such a miserable companion.

As an ordained priest, I should have been able to throw off this mood of depression. Devotional books which I had read at theological college often referred to "the dark night of the soul": but it was a state from which the Saints of God arose with a new inner strength, a new vision of their calling, a new courage. Unlike them, I saw no light at the end of the tunnel. Darkness enveloped me.

Unable to read for more than a limited period, I was left with too much time to think and too many thoughts on my mind. How could I snap out of this mood of hopelessness? Had the time come to get away from the East End? I found myself repeating the first lines of Thomas Merton's prayer:

I have no idea where I am going. I do not see the road ahead of me. I cannot know for certain where it will end. Nor do I really know myself, and the fact that I am following Your will does not mean that I am actually doing so.

But I was unable to reach the certainty of Merton's conclusion:

But I believe the desire to please You *does* please You . . . I hope that I will never do anything apart from that desire. And I know that if I do this You will lead me by the right road . . . Therefore will I trust You always though I may seem to be lost . . . I will not fear, for You are ever with me.

For the moment, I was unable to make any decisions of my own, complying automatically with suggestions from Diana or Eliza Jones. Enthusiasm had vanished and even the children could not bring back any joy to living.

No doubt Diana and I should have followed her father's advice and taken a holiday well away from London's East End. But, rightly or wrongly, we decided to resume our life at St. Mildred's in the hope that our personal sorrow would be buried in the daily round that kept us both busy. Certainly we were helped by the sympathy of our neighbours, many of them previously unknown to us—people in the shops and the school and members of the St. Mildred's congregation. Sad news travels quickly in the East End.

Of course we had our lighter moments, too. One evening Diana invited the Bloxhams to evening tea and cake at the vicarage, coffee having no place in the Bloxham diet: and Stevie was persuaded to retell his story, as once he had told it to the police at Clerkenwell.

"It was like this, yer see." This was a typical Stevie opening. "I was out on the late night run in the West End, just as I'd told the wife. We do pretty well out of these night-club gents—very generous, open-'anded like. About two in the mornin' I decided to pack it up. There am I, full of cash an' contentment and whistlin 'ome sweet 'ome, when two Middle East blokes come out of a gambling joint and ask for a lift to one o' them posh 'otels at London airport. Luck's in, Stevie, I says to meself: and sure enough, two hours later I'm startin' on the long road 'ome with another twenty green backs in the purse.

"Then, would yer believe it, just as I wheel onto the M4, two gents give me a shout from the roadside. Car's broken down, they say. What about a lift to town? We'll pay you good. 'Op in, says I, reckonin' it's a right bonanza for Stevie— but then I smell somethin' suspicious. First these two characters shove a couple o' suitcases in the back—lots of fares do that, yer know, 'opin' to save the baggage charge. But on a long journey? Not bloody likely.

Next I see their car's a pretty nifty Volvo Estate. Break-down? 'Undred to one against. Now if they'd run out of gas, that would be a more likely tale. See? 'Owever I'm not lookin' for trouble at four o'clock on a lonely road, so I notes the Volvo number and off we go.

"I can't quite 'ear what these gents are sayin' in the back of the cab but they sound as if they're not too 'appy with a lad what ought to 'ave met them earlier on. Funny, I thinks to meself, very funny. You'd best do somethin' abaht it, old cock: or someone will be after you. So when I've dumped the fares at the Aldersgate entrance to the Barbican, I takes their cash—many thanks, driver, no change required—and makes for the police station.

"But it seems I've put the cops onto somethin' a bloomin' sight more interestin' than a stolen car. They tell me I'll 'ave to tell the story again to some detective chap and the fingerprint men start creepin' all over my bus. By the time I'm clear, 'aving enjoyed a good free breakfast and a nap in a nice armchair, it's well into the morning. So the cops agree to let Jane know what's been 'appenin' to the old man: and I drive west to pick up the midday business.

"One way an' another, I'm not 'ome till the evening. It's only then I learns that one of the swine 'as dropped this billydoo through our letterbox. Cor, 'ow's that for a night out?" Stevie paused. "And, knock me down, it's only next mornin' I sees the *Mirror* 'eadlines 'Parson in Pub Punch-up'. What a tale of woe. But I tell you somethin', Mrs. Eveleigh. Yer 'usband's quite an 'ero round 'ere—won 'is spurs, yer might say. Most of us are on the side of law an' order, yer know: and we like to 'ave Mr. Eveleigh on our side."

For a further month, we soldiered on at St. Mildred's, coping with the work as best we could. But the inescapable fact remained—as the Archdeacon told us in his forthright way—that we needed a change of scene. We'd been doing too much and must take a complete rest before starting a fresh assignment. We were not to worry about St. Mildred's: the Rural Dean would arrange for the Sunday Services, and Eliza was fully competent to phone a neighbouring parson concerning any case that might present itself at the vicarage. A very forceful, practical man was the Archdeacon —you can understand why Diana and I identified him with Trollope's Barchester character.

"No ifs and buts, Richard," he concluded. "You and Diana are to take a complete rest and I think you'll be happiest if you take the two children with you. In fact, I've reserved provisional accommodation for you at a conference house near Tunbridge Wells where you can rely on good food, good beds, a good library and a measure of quiet. Good luck. And for Heaven's sake, try to stop blaming yourself over this unfortunate business. You've done a thundering good job at St. Mildred's, you and Diana. We're very grateful to you."

Somewhere behind Grantly's powerful frame lay a warm heart and a lot of common sense.

Those weeks away from responsibility did us all good. Our first week was spent at Broadstairs with Rosie Ashcroft—my first visit to 37 Cherry Tree Close since that ghastly Dickens evening with Keith Figgis. Rosie's elder boy was in the RAF and the younger in his last year at Oxford: and she was happy enough to join our small family on our beach picnics when she wasn't teaching. She also brought us up-to-date about Cliff's End. Harold Goldworthy, it seemed, had finally decided to close the school and sell the property for building. Who could blame him? He had earned his long-overdue retirement. There was no family succession and the minimum figure he could expect from a property company would exceed ten years' profits from the school—and provide him with an excellent annuity, too.

One thing was certain. The old man would see to it that all his staff were cared for. Rosie was already making plans to sell her Broadstairs house and find a place close to Canterbury where she would find better openings for her musical and artistic interests.

Our stay at the Clergy Retreat near Tunbridge Wells was equally relaxed; but was chiefly notable for one memorable day. On that golden day in autumn, we left Nicholas and Philippa in the charge of a girl attached to the Conference Centre, and set off in the Morris for a day's outing to

Leeds Castle. The royal palace fortress was as beautiful as when we had seen it on the last day of our honeymoon—its battlements mirrored in the surrounding water and its Gloriette and Royal Chantry speaking out of the past of chivalry and a king's love for his queen.

Once again we climbed to the little height of land above the water meadows and gazed spell-bound upon this man-made jewel, glittering in the sunshine, with the peace of Kentish woods and water for its setting. Surely in its perfection it was part of God's creation. There, as we had done eight years previously, we enjoyed our picnic lunch, and afterwards lay in each other's arms, unconscious of the passing of present time, aware only of a bird singing to his mate and the eternal rhythm of the river.

There, too, beneath the trees with the sunshine winking through the leaves, we made love together as once we had made love in the vale of Ockenham. There was no diminishing of our love. But now it was my hands which loosed Diana's clothes and explored her body, I who thrust into her and she who received me with a passion too long restrained by sorrow. We joined each other in a climax of love, as if nature's need for new life commanded us to do so.

Later—much later—we roused ourselves and, like children on a treasure hunt, drove the few miles to Leeds village. We discovered beside a small stream the sorry stones left by Henry VIII's commissioners of destruction to remind visitors of de Crêvecoeur's great Priory of St. Mary and St. Nicholas: and our spirits soared as we entered the church at the top of the hill, and stood by the Norman font where, in our imagining, a Prior's illegitimate son had once been baptized and christened "Nicholas Maidstone".

Happy as any two lovers can be, we drove back down the hill, and across the Weald of Kent until we reached our temporary home. The children were already in bed and asleep when we returned to join the other residents for the evening meal.

After supper came the extraordinary sequel to our day. Taking coffee in the lounge, I casually picked up the current issue of the *Church Times*. Glancing through the clerical vacancy notices which appear towards the end of that very well-edited paper my eyes suddenly lighted upon the following advertisement:

The Parish of St. Dunstan, Ockenham, Nr. Canterbury

———

This Benefice falls vacant 1 January 1968. Farming community. Modern vicarage. Suitable for Incumbent with young family.

———

Application forms available from the Patron of the Living: Major P. Mortimer-Wotton, The Manor House, Ockenham, Nr. Canterbury, Kent.

I passed the paper to Diana. We read the notice again as if our eyes could not believe the printed word.

There was, of course, nothing we could do that night, though we had no doubt as to our course of action. For the moment, our hopes were a private secret between us. When we went to bed I opened the prayer

269

book in our room and turned to the collect for the second Sunday after Easter. Together we prayed: "O God of Peace, Make us perfect to do your will, and work in us that which is well-pleasing in your sight." It was, I suppose, the measure of our commitment.

5

WHAT followed was, I truly believe, preordained. I wrote to Major Philip Mortimer-Wotton, applying for the Living of St. Dunstan's, Ockenham. I persuaded John Spencer, who had friends all over the place, to act as my sponsor: and I understood that "Archdeacon Grantly" was prepared to speak in my favour.

I had no idea how much competition I was likely to face. But I meant to leave as little as possible to chance: "time spent on reconnaissance is seldom wasted" was one of the few basic truths I remembered from my two years' National Service. So, as soon as I had received, completed and posted the application forms, I motored down to Ockenham with Diana and the children.

Our first call was on Miss Millie. When we pulled up at her thatched cottage, we found her in conversation with an old lady whom she introduced to us as Miss Morgan —"Miss Gwynedd Morgan whose brother you've met in the village." I recalled the name at once. She was the sister of the garage man, Evan Morgan. She was the Major's old nurse who had agreed to look after the *bambino* on that Christmas evening when the Italians from the Great House had been my fellow guests at Ted and Luisa's party at the Wotton Arms. She had also been instrumental in fixing up my fortnight's stay at Millicent Taylor's cottage. But this was my first meeting with Gwynedd—and, indeed, my first meeting with Miss Millie since my posting to St. Mildred's.

The old ladies expressed great interest in my reasons for this preliminary visit. We'd like the Major, they both assured us: and then took it in turns to inform Diana and me of the Major's likes and dislikes. Between them, they presented us with a most surprising picture of the occupant of the Great House.

"Takes a real interest in St. Dunstan's, just as his dear grandmother used to do."

"Thinks of it as the focal point of the village."

"Won't hold any office in the church,

though he never misses Communion at eight o'clock."

"Hates people talking about his Rights: says the Church of England should stop kow-towing to rich landowners."

"Says paying deference to the rich is the quickest way to empty a village church in these post-war days."

"Insists the church belongs equally to all of us."

"Only Pharisees permit a 'pecking order' in a congregation." The old ladies were clearly quoting verbatim from the Major's "obiter dicta" and Diana and I felt ourselves instinctively warming to the man.

With the skill of women accustomed to handling children, neither took any apparent notice of Nicholas and Philippa exploring Miss Millie's garden. Only when Gwynedd Morgan took her leave did she give any indication that the children had not been unobserved. She said,

"It's nice to see your children are such good friends. One day, perhaps, they may like to visit my little house and meet my cat and some of the animals in the farm by the Oast House." And with that, the old lady said goodbye and hurried on her way.

Miss Millie smiled indulgently at her departing friend.

"Gwynedd is marvellous with children, Richard: but you must take what she says about the Major with a grain of salt. You see, he's been her first love ever since his mother died. Philip was a little boy of three at the time. But she *does* know how he thinks: and he often visits her house. And he really *is* different from other landowners round here. Parson, ploughman, peer—he treats them all the same. He judges them as he judges apples: good, bad or tasteless. Their size is unimportant."

Later, we gained the same impression from the retiring incumbent when we called to inspect the vicarage. The house blended well with the older houses round the church. It had a garden gate into the churchyard and had been built on land presented to the church by the Major after the war. It was, we were told, a sort of practical thank-offering for his safe return to Ockenham.

The Vicar also confirmed what I had earlier heard from Ted Baker that, since the war, the Mortimer-Wotton estate had been formed into a private company, in which the church as well as the tenant farmers and senior farm workers held shares carrying the same voting rights as those held by members of the family. On our return to London Diana began to speak of him as Philippe Egalité. He really *was* different, as Miss Millie had said.

In due course I travelled to Canterbury for a long and searching interview with the Bishop of Dover. But it was clear that the final decision about St. Dunstan's rested with the Patron of the Living. Apparently, negotiations were in train for the appointment to be taken over by Canterbury, but long and detailed legal processes were involved. So long as the Mortimer-Wottons were concerned with the Gift of the Living, the head of the family would take the closest personal interest in the appointment. Finally, arrangements were made by phone for me to visit Ockenham Manor in the following week.

On the day fixed for my appointment Diana and I left London early. Somehow, I felt an overwhelming compulsion to visit the church before I kept my date with the Major.

There was nobody near St. Dunstan's

when I drove up to the lychgate. We locked the car and walked past the yew trees lining the path to the south door. We entered the silent, unlit church and walked hand in hand up the aisle towards the rail before the altar. It was almost like a marriage ceremony without witnesses.

Or were we without witnesses? As we knelt together before the altar, we were conscious of a great stillness. We remained silent . . . listening . . . seeking total communion . . . total commitment to our purpose.

We both felt very small and very humble. God, we knew, was beyond man's understanding and outside the concept of space or time, but his spirit was surely present in this ancient church that mortal men and women had raised to his glory. A shaft of sunlight, shining through a small side window in the chancel, brought sudden illumination to the cross in front of us. And I found myself repeating in the sixteenth-century English of the Authorised Version the opening verse of the twelfth chapter of Hebrews:

Seeing we also are compassed about with

so great a cloud of witnesses, let us lay aside every weight, and the sin which doth so easily beset us, and let us run with patience the race that is set before us . . .

We left the church, hand in hand as we had entered it. Diana paused in the porch at the south door, looked at the long list of incumbents and kissed me. As she turned towards the car, she said,

"Good luck, my darling. It will be nice if Richard Eveleigh's name appears on the Honours Board."

I watched her move with her light, quick footsteps towards the lychgate. Then I crossed the churchyard to a stile which joined a field path leading to the park of the Great House. As I walked across the open ground, my mind went back over the past thirteen years. To the dream in this churchyard and the vision of the suffering priest. To my mother's disclosure about my birth, forced out of her in this church and my stupid reaction to the truth, which only Rosie Ashcroft knew about. To the recurring appearance of this mediaeval priest and the lonely Christmas walk which led me to

Number 84 and John Spencer and back to Diana. To my honeymoon with Diana here in Ockenham, and to Miss Millie's story of John Frebody and the Holy Maid. To the moment of decision in Victoria Park and to my curacies in two places once familiar to the two priests of Ockenham . . . and back again to my own mistakes and my feelings of guilt. But now, I reassured myself, I was out of the past and into the present. I was reminded of T. S. Eliot's lines:

> What might have been and what has
> been,
> Point to one end, which is always
> present.

As I left the field path to enter the beech avenue leading to the Major's house, I was buoyed up with a new confidence such as I had never before experienced.

I was five minutes early for the appointment and was conducted to a room at the south-west corner of the mansion. A window on the west wall of the room looked up the valley, and a second window faced north, providing a view across the lake

278

towards the church on its little hill beyond the Canterbury road. Fitted book shelves, rising to five feet, surrounded the room, allowing space above the books for various family photographs.

As the clock struck the hour, Philip Mortimer-Wotton entered the room. He was accompanied by another Labrador—a younger version of the old bitch we had met thirteen years earlier on our journey in the black Rolls to the Wotton Arms.

The major was at once recognisable for what he was—a typical ex-Guards officer, tall and well built, with clear blue eyes, a military moustache and fair hair going grey. He was wearing a country tweed suit which carried the unmistakable stamp of Savile Row. But as Millicent Taylor and Gwynedd Morgan had told us, there was no pomposity, no hint of superiority about him. I could see him treating anybody he chanced to meet with the same friendly, good-humoured courtesy. I could understand why he commanded equal loyalty from the Bakers, the Morgans and the Italian servants.

He spoke in short, abrupt sentences, wasting neither time nor words.

"Good morning," he said. "Please sit down, Mr. Eveleigh. Do you smoke? No? Nor do I. Thank you for arriving on time —I appreciate punctuality."

He seated himself at the desk opposite me and took some papers from a file in front of him.

"Richard Eveleigh," he was reading, half to himself, from some notes in his neat hand-writing. "Richard Brooke Eveleigh, Clerk in Holy Orders. Age thirty-seven. Education, Dulwich and Oxford. Married, two children. Ordained Southwark, 1964. Has held curacies in Blackheath and St. Mildred's E1. Formerly schoolmaster at Kent preparatory school, office worker with property company and lay assistant in Wapping Mission . . ." Occasionally during the reading he looked up to be sure I agreed the facts. Once he paused to pat the Labrador beside him.

"Hum . . . seems to fit the bill," he murmured: and suddenly he jerked out, "Haven't I seen you before, Padré?"

"Yes, sir. You once gave my mother and me a lift to the Wotton Arms. And you may have seen me and my wife at the early service in the parish church."

"That's right. I remember now. And you know Ted Baker down at the Wotton Arms?"

"Yes, sir. I first discovered Ockenham back in 1954 when I was a rather unsuccessful schoolmaster. I've loved the village and the valley ever since. In fact, my wife and I spent our honeymoon at Ted Baker's inn."

The Major looked up at me and I detected the suspicion of a smile on his face —a sense of humour in his eyes.

"Unsuccessful schoolmaster, eh? And more recently you've engaged in a punch-up in Clerkenwell, what? Not to worry. I got the story from your Archdeacon who took lunch with me at White's. His name escapes me, but he was good company and enjoyed the club claret. Told me all about your activities in East London. Didn't think your recent encounter with criminals should disqualify you from running a country parish." The Major smiled more broadly. "I told him we could supply a few criminals in these parts too."

"The Archdeacon has certainly been a good friend to me and my wife over these last few weeks," I said, and added cautiously, "and he will no doubt have told you that, according to the doctors, there should be no after-effects from my concussion."

My voice must have trailed away for the Major said,

"Speak up, do you mind? I ought to have told you earlier. I'm a bit deaf."

I could have kicked myself, for I'm sure Miss Millie or Ted Baker had told me of this disability; but it didn't seem to matter. The Major proceeded with a fusillade of short, sharp questions which made me feel for a moment as inadequate as a Sandhurst cadet hoping to win acceptance into a crack regiment.

Suddenly, the interrogation came to an end. The Major closed his file and put it in one of the desk drawers.

"Sorry to seem a little formal, Mr. Eveleigh," he said. "But I like to follow the same drill on these occasions with each candidate. Actually, I've already decided the job is yours, if you'll take it. Any questions?"

His concluding words hit me so suddenly that surprise at the speed of his decision and sheer excitement left me speechless. He rose from the desk laughing.

"May I take it, Padré, that silence denotes consent? Come, let's go and drink to St. Dunstan's future health. You were very wise, you know, to employ Millicent Taylor as your advocate. That marvellous little woman carries the same authority with me as she did when she taught me to read and write at the village school. She may be only two jampots high but she carries an Archdeacon's weight as a sponsor.

"Which reminds me, Padré—you've another local supporter in these parts. Young Piers Bovill, Lord Eglemont's son, has been over here, studying the way we manage the Ockenham Farm Co-operative. He and Hugh Dickinson hope to run a similar scheme at Monteagle if the family and their legal advisers can be persuaded. A good lad, Piers. When I told him of your application he fairly sang your praises, if you can apply such a phrase to a boy who has suffered from a stammer as long as I've known him. But enough of this talk. It's time for a drink."

We crossed the hall to a light and spacious room, with the Labrador confidently leading the way. The Major filled two glasses from a sherry decanter.

"Here's to your very good health," he said, "and now, as I promised Miss Millie, I will show you two exhibits which have always appealed to her historian's imagination."

First he handed me an exquisite sixteenth-century miniature—painted in Antwerp, artist unknown, but clearly depicting John Frebody's strong, bold face, with the cross of St. John of Jerusalem just visible at his shoulder.

Then, as casually as if he were asking me to examine a new book just arrived from Hatchards, he handed me a slim leather-bound volume which he had extracted from a protective case.

I opened the binding: and there, open before my eyes, were some pages of the Bible set out in an exquisite monkish script. I turned to the last page and read a rather uncertain signature: "Hoc scripsit Nicholas Maidstone." I stared at it in amazement.

"Interesting, isn't it?" the Major was saying. "Had it identified by the Bible Society. It's the First Epistle of St. John from the English translation of the Bible, commissioned by John Wycliff and known as the Hereford Bible. Handwritten, of course, before printing was invented. You'll find that chap, Nicholas Maidstone, on the list of vicars in the church—he was a contemporary of Wycliff and mixed up, some say, in the Peasants' Revolt."

"But it's marvellous," I blurted out, "absolutely marvellous."

"Yes, I often look at it," the Major continued. "I suppose our Nicholas didn't have time to write out more than a few pages—still, he chose the best bit. Look at this," and he turned to a page where he had placed a ribbon marker. "The meaning's clear enough even if the spelling is wobbly and the punctuation non-existent."

Moost dere brithen love we togide for charite is of God and ech that lovith his brother is born of God, He that lovith not knoweth not God for God is charite.

I continued to stare at it.

"But where did you find it?" I asked. "Is it a family heirloom?"

"No," he said. "It came into my grandmother's hands after the First War. An old cabinet-maker—he was churchwarden at the time—found it in the church, in an old chest in the priest's room above the south door. Sad story, really. The pious old chap who discovered it had a son who put a girl from Ashford in the family way. My grandmother arranged for the child's adoption and got the boy away to Canada. We've since heard that he was among the Canadians killed in the Dieppe raid. But the old man—he had a name rather like yours, Padré, but spelt it Eveley, and claimed descent from the great mediaeval builder, Henry Yvele—was so upset over the affair that he moved away from the village. He died many years ago but insisted on leaving the manuscript with us. My grandmother had it bound in order to preserve it."

I continued to stare at the text, hoping against hope that the Major would never know the stunning effect of his casual story about the Hereford Bible.

Here, in the Great House at Ockenham, the moment of truth had arrived. I suddenly realised that Tom Eveleigh must have known my natural father's surname at the time of my adoption; and struck by the similarity between Eveley and Eveleigh, used his artist's imagination to invent the story of yeoman origins which my mother always tried to discount. Now I knew for a certainty that I, Richard Eveleigh, was by natural affinity a native of Ockenham.

A few minutes later Philip Mortimer-Wotton accompanied me to the front door.

"I try to gear myself to change," he said, "but some things manage to survive, thank God."

I wasn't sure whether he was thinking of the manuscript, St. Dunstan's, or the wider world.

"Yes," I agreed, "your Hereford Bible belongs, like the parish church of Ockenham, to the present and future as well as the past."

"That's right," he said. Then, as his way was, he snapped back into the present.

"No car, Padré? Can I give you a lift?"

"Thank you, sir. But it's only a short walk to the Wotton Arms where my wife is waiting for me."

"Of course, of course. Next time we meet, you must introduce me to Mrs. Eveleigh and your children. I look forward to meeting them. Meanwhile, I'll be in touch with Canterbury and write to you as soon as possible about fixing the date of your Institution. I'm delighted that you already know some of the people here. I hope you'll be very happy."

We said goodbye. With the Labrador motionless beside him, he watched me walk down the drive. I know because just before the beech trees hid the house from view, I looked back to see his tall commanding figure still standing in front of the Great House, looking towards St. Dunstan's.

I hurried down the drive, my heart bursting with excitement and my imagination filling the place with people. People from history, saints and sinners, Mortimers and Wottons, the long line of incumbents who had served their course in this place . . . people of today whom I was still to meet . . . a world without end.

I wanted to run, to dance, to shout for joy. I emerged from the Lodge gates onto the Canterbury road. Playing in the village street were the children just released from school. And behind them I saw Diana coming towards me, her eyes sparkling, her arms outstretched in welcome.

"I know, I know," she cried.

"You are right," I said. "The dreams have come true. And now I even know who I am, as well as where we are going."

THE END

The full story of Ockenham and Philip Mortimer-Wootton may be found in John Attenborough's earlier novel "One Man's Inheritance".

GUIDE
TO THE COLOUR CODING
OF
ULVERSCROFT BOOKS

Many of our readers have written to us expressing their appreciation for the way in which our colour coding has assisted them in selecting the Ulverscroft books of their choice. To remind everyone of our colour coding— this is as follows:

BLACK COVERS
Mysteries

*

BLUE COVERS
Romances

*

RED COVERS
Adventure Suspense and General Fiction

*

ORANGE COVERS
Westerns

*

GREEN COVERS
Non-Fiction